Books by Ed Dunlop

The Terrestria Chronicles
The Sword, the Ring, and the Parchment
The Quest for Seven Castles
The Search for Everyman
The Crown of Kuros
The Dragon's Egg
The Golden Lamps
The Great War

Tales from Terrestria
The Quest for Thunder Mountain
The Golden Dagger
The Return of the Dagger
The Isle of Dragons

Jed Cartwright Adventure Series
The Midnight Escape
The Lost Gold Mine
The Comanche Raiders
The Lighthouse Mystery
The Desperate Slave
The Midnight Rustlers

The Young Refugees Series
Escape to Liechtenstein
The Search for the Silver Eagle
The Incredible Rescues

Sherlock Jones Detective Series
Sherlock Jones and the Assassination Plot
Sherlock Jones and the Willoughby Bank Robbery
Sherlock Jones and the Missing Diamond
Sherlock Jones and the Phantom Airplane
Sherlock Jones and the Hidden Coins
Sherlock Jones and the Odyssey Mystery

The 1,000-Mile Journey

Tales from Terrestria: Book One

*An allegory
by Ed Dunlop*

cross & crown
PUBLISHING
RINGGOLD, GEORGIA

©2008 Ed Dunlop   All rights reserved

www.TalesOfCastles.com
Cover Art by Laura Lea Sencabaugh and Wayne Coley

The Quest for Thunder Mountain : an allegory / by Ed Dunlop.
Dunlop, Ed.
[Ringgold, Ga.] : Cross and Crown Publishing, c2008
203 p. ; 22 cm.
Tales from Terrestria Bk. 1
Dewey Call # 813.54
ISBN 978-0-9785523-8-1

When Gavin's career comes to an abrupt end, the talented young minstrel learns that King Emmanuel has plans for him—plans that promise life and purpose. But Gavin must make a difficult quest to a mysterious mountain.

Dunlop, Ed.
Middle ages juvenile fiction.
Christian life juvenile fiction.
Allegories.
Fantasy

Printed and bound in the United States of America

*That my heart
would find delight
in the will of my King*

I delight to do thy will,
O my God:
yea, thy law is
within my heart.

— *Psalm 40:8*

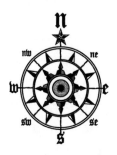

Chapter One

Lightning slashed across the darkening skies and thunder boomed angrily in reply as a black coach sped recklessly down a steep slope toward a small Terrestrian village. The coachman, a tall, gaunt figure dressed in solid black, hunched lower into his greatcoat. The wind howled and moaned like a creature in pain. Oaks and boxwoods lining the narrow roadway writhed and swayed as if dancing to silent music. The blackness of night threatened as the storm raced toward the little town.

The coach swayed dangerously when it reached the foot of the hill. Racing into a curve, the speeding coach careened recklessly to one side and then at the last possible moment righted itself. It slowed for an even tighter curve.

The storm arrived suddenly. The rain crashed down with a vengeance as the darkness of night abruptly descended like a black curtain. The ominous, sodden clouds above the sleepy village abruptly unloaded upon the unsuspecting town, releasing their burdens as if sliced open with a knife. Rain fell in torrents, pummeling the hillside and then flowing down toward the village in muddy streams and rivulets. The coachman was immediately drenched by the violent downpour, and he cursed bitterly. A white-hot bolt of lightning illuminated the valley.

At that moment, the door to the coach flew open. "Please, sire!" a frantic voice pleaded, and then a human figure tumbled from the open doorway to land sprawling in the thickets at the roadside. The coach sped on and was swallowed by the blackness of the night.

With a cry of dismay the figure at the roadside leaped to his feet, but the coach was gone. Immediately drenched by the unrelenting downpour, the hapless person looked around desperately. An observer would have noted that he was disheveled but well-dressed, shaking with cold and fear, and that he was a young man about to cross that line that separates youth from manhood. "King Emmanuel, help me," he cried in desperation. "What am I to do now?"

With an explosion of sound and a shock wave that made every nerve in the young man's body tingle, a fiery bolt of lightning struck the hillside less than fifty paces from where he stood, stunning and paralyzing him. The resulting crash of thunder was so powerful that the concussion of sound knocked him to the ground. But in that brief instant that the hillside was illuminated brighter than a hundred daylights, his probing eyes spotted a crude shelter, an abandoned hay wagon. It wasn't much, but it would provide a slight reprieve from the sheer violence of the storm.

He crawled toward it, and then, regaining the full use of his limbs, rose to his feet and staggered toward it. The wind howled and gusted, throwing handfuls of rain into his face as if determined to keep him from reaching the wagon. A racking cough shook his slender body and he shivered uncontrollably. With an unearthly cry that was somewhere between a moan and a sob, he literally fell into the mud beneath the wagon.

The youth crawled forward and then curled up against the broken front axle. Lacking a cloak or coat to protect himself from the brutality of the tempest, he simply raised trembling hands to shield his face. A prolonged fit of coughing shook his entire body. "My lord, Emmanuel," he moaned, "help me! What am I to do now?"

Lightning stabbed at the hillside, the valley, and the defenseless village, striking again and again without mercy as if trying to obliterate the landscape. High on the hillside, a mighty oak took a direct hit and exploded in a barrage of flying limbs and bark. Thunder rocked the valley, echoing and re-echoing until the youth clutched his ears in pain. It sounded as if Terrestria was being destroyed.

In the midst of the swirling maelstrom of rain, wind, lightning, and thunder, a lone yellow light appeared, bobbing and weaving erratically as it traveled toward the decaying hay wagon.

The wind abruptly ceased its shrieking and the downpour lessened considerably. Darkness reigned as the lightning stopped and the thunder was silenced, creating an unexpected calm. The youth raised his head.

At that instant, a fiery bolt of lightning struck an outcropping of granite less than ten paces from the wagon. The ledge shattered, hurling tiny shards of rock to strike the face and neck of the youth, and a shock wave of intense heat and energy seared his face and throat. Stunned and temporarily blinded, he dropped his head to the protection of the cold mud beneath him.

When a warm glow of yellow light caught his attention, he raised his head and then cried out in terror. The white hair and wrinkled skin of an old man's face had appeared just inches from his own. Disembodied and without definite form, the face floated in the darkness of the storm. "What are you?" the youth cried out in fear. "Have you come to destroy me?"

A hand touched his shoulder and the terrified youth recoiled in panic, striking his head on the iron rim of the wagon wheel and nearly knocking himself unconscious. Stunned and disoriented, he struggled to scramble from beneath the wagon.

"Gavin," a calm voice called, and the youth realized that he was in the grip of two powerful hands. "Gavin, it's all right! I won't hurt you. It's all right, lad."

The youth stopped struggling and cowered in the mud as he awaited the inevitable. "What do you want with me?"

"It's all right, Gavin," the quiet voice assured him. "I've come to help you."

Gavin raised his head. "Who are—?" A fit of coughing interrupted his words. "Who are you?"

"Just a friend who wants to help you, lad."

"How—how do you know my name?" The light moved, and the youth could now see the form of an old man kneeling in the mud beside the wagon. He sighed with relief. This was no evil apparition or banshee, just an old man with a lantern.

Strong hands lifted him to a sitting position and his wet, trembling body was suddenly engulfed in the warm folds of a dry cloak. "Follow me, Gavin," the quiet voice said. "Let's get you inside, out of this dreadful storm." The old man's eyes searched his face. "Are you ready to make a run for it?"

Gavin nodded. "I'll follow your light."

The old man's arm slipped around him, scooping him from beneath the wagon and lifting him to his feet in one motion. "We'll go together."

The intensity of the tempest seemed to increase as Gavin and the old man hurried through the darkness of the night. Peering anxiously through the crashing wind and the slashing rain, Gavin could barely see the ground in the feeble glow from the lantern, but his companion seemed to know where he was going. He led Gavin through a steep ravine, across a little stream, and into a forest that sheltered them somewhat from the full violence of the storm. At last, the old man paused and lifted the lantern, and Gavin could see that they had reached the weather-beaten door of a humble cottage.

"Come in out of the storm, lad," the old man invited, lifting the latch and pushing open the door. Gavin threw himself across the threshold.

As the old man closed the door, the feeble light from the lantern seemed to increase a hundredfold. A cheerful fire blazed on the hearth and the little table before it was set with two steaming bowls of porridge. Gavin stared. It was almost as if he had been expected.

The strong hands of the old man peeled the cloak and the cold, wet outer clothing from Gavin's shivering body. "Come," his host invited, "stand before the fire and warm up. You must be chilled to the bone." As he spoke, he wrapped a warm blanket around Gavin's shoulders. Gavin bent over in a prolonged fit of coughing.

The warmth from the blazing fire slowly crept into Gavin's bones. "Sire, I thank you for rescuing me," he said gratefully. "But for you…"

"Don't talk now," his host admonished him, handing him a steaming mug. "Drink this. It will warm your insides and soothe that cough of yours."

Gavin took a huge gulp of the hot cider. The warm drink flowed through his being like liquid fire, warming and strengthening him. He took a deep breath and then another big gulp. "Sire, thank you," he whispered. "But for you I would have died."

Several moments later, when warmth had returned to Gavin's aching body and he was dressed in a warm, dry robe, the old man gestured toward the table. "Have a seat, Gavin. A little hot porridge will do you good."

"Sire, who are you?" Gavin demanded. "How do you know my name?" He gazed around the cottage. "You have hot cider and porridge ready, and a robe just my size and...sire, if I didn't know better, I'd say that you were expecting me. Who are you, anyway? How...how did you know that I was coming and would need your help?"

The old man turned slowly. His face was calm and peaceful and his clear gray eyes sparkled with friendliness. "I make it my business to know these things, lad."

"But who are you, sire?"

"Eat," the man said, gently leading him to the table. "We can talk over our porridge."

Within moments Gavin discovered that the porridge was absolutely delicious. Once he started he couldn't seem to get the spoon to his mouth fast enough. Warmth flowed through him and he luxuriated in the feeling.

"I am a nobleman in the service of King Emmanuel," his host said, when he and Gavin were halfway through the simple meal. "My name is Wisdom, or, as some call me, Sir Wisdom. I was simply sent to help you in your time of need." The clear gray eyes studied Gavin's face, and a sad smile crossed the man's countenance. "You took a rather mean tumble from that coach, lad."

"Sir Entertainment threw me out," Gavin retorted angrily. "I am a minstrel and I have been traveling with him, singing and playing for the lords and their ladies at the various castles. When I became ill and lost my voice, he threw me out like an old shoe!"

Sir Wisdom's eyes met Gavin's and the youth felt as if the old man could see right into his soul. "You have discovered for yourself just how treacherous a master Argamor can be, did you not? Aye, Argamor will use you, and then he casts you aside when you are no longer useful to him. Like an old shoe, as you put it."

Gavin paused with the spoon halfway to his mouth "Argamor? But I wasn't serving Argamor, sire."

"Then whom were you serving?" Sir Wisdom asked.

Gavin shrugged and swallowed the spoonful of porridge. "I wasn't serving anyone, sire."

"We all serve someone or something," the nobleman corrected. "Whom were you serving?"

"Then I would have to say that I was serving myself. I was singing simply for the chance to travel and become known, and to make some money."

"So you weren't doing it for King Emmanuel's honor and glory—which means that you were serving Argamor."

"How can you say that, sire?"

"You weren't serving Emmanuel, were you?"

"Not really, but I wouldn't say that I was serving Argamor, sire. Argamor is the sworn enemy of His Majesty and I would never serve him."

"'He that is not with me is against me; and he that gathereth not with me scattereth.' His Majesty's own words, lad."

Gavin sighed and was thoughtful for a moment. "Then perhaps I was serving Argamor, though I did not realize it."

"There is forgiveness with His Majesty," Sir Wisdom said softly.

Gavin nodded and fell silent.

When the simple meal was finished, Gavin thanked his host and then arose from the table and took a seat before the fire. He reached out and checked his wet clothing which Sir Wisdom had hung to dry upon the cooking crane. "Already!" he exclaimed.

The old man looked up from his task of clearing the table. "Your clothing is dry, I take it?"

"Aye, sire. That was mighty fast."

"It's a hot fire." He studied Gavin's face. "And what are your plans now, may I ask?"

Gavin hung his head. "I have no plans, sire. This all happened so quickly." He sighed as he watched the crackling fire. Just then, a burning log collapsed, sending a shower of brilliant sparks up the chimney. The youth turned and looked at Sir Wisdom, and the old man saw the unspoken plea in his eyes. "I—I suppose that I will change back into my own clothing and try to find a place to spend the night."

"Find a place to spend the night, lad?" Sir Wisdom stiffened and drew himself up to his full height as if he were offended by the words. "And what is wrong with these accommodations, may I ask?"

"Nothing, s-sire," Gavin stammered. "I would love to stay here. I—I just was afraid to ask, sire."

The old man grinned. "If you tried to step out into that storm I would stop you, lad. You're spending the night here. I'm already planning on it."

Relief flooded over Gavin. "Thank you, sire."

Sir Wisdom placed a basin on the table, poured water from a pitcher, and began to wash the utensils from the meal. As he worked, he watched Gavin. The youth sat by the fireplace with shoulders slumped, head down, and a woeful look on his young face. "What's on your mind?" he asked, though he knew exactly what Gavin was thinking.

"What am I to do?" Gavin lamented. "I will stay with you tonight, sire, and I do appreciate your hospitality, but what am I to do tomorrow? I have no home and no way to provide for myself. This all happened so suddenly."

"His Majesty has plans for you," Sir Wisdom said quietly. Gavin's head shot up. "What do you mean by that, sire?"

"Emmanuel knows your needs, lad. I see that you have no chain of iniquity or weight of guilt, so I know that you have been set free by Emmanuel and that you are one of his children. He knows what is best for you, and he has a plan for your life. What you need to do now is concentrate on finding that plan."

"If Emmanuel has a plan for me, why did he allow me to be thrown from the coach in the middle of a terrible storm? I was doing fine as a minstrel. Life was good enough, and I enjoyed what I was doing. But now it seems that it all has been taken from me."

"He took it from you so that you would look to him," the old man replied quietly.

A puzzled expression appeared on Gavin's face.

"You said that life was 'good enough', yet Emmanuel wants you to live an abundant life, not just a life that is 'good enough'. His plans for you far exceed any plans that you could have had, and yet you were satisfied with the meager existence that you knew. This afternoon, before you were tossed so unceremoniously from that coach, would you have been interested in learning Emmanuel's will for you?"

Gavin shrugged.

"Perhaps not," Sir Wisdom answered for him. "You didn't see your need for him; you were doing just fine on your own. But now, after being tossed out like a piece of garbage, you are willing to admit your need of him, are you not? Emmanuel now has your attention, and I dare say that you are willing to listen."

He smiled as if he knew something that Gavin did not. "I think you are ready for the quest."

"The quest, sire? What is the quest?"

"The quest for Thelema Mountain," the old man replied vaguely, smiling that mysterious smile again.

"Where is Thelema Mountain?"

"Let's get some sleep, shall we?" Sir Wisdom replied. "I'll tell you about Thelema Mountain in the morning. I do believe that you are about to embark on a quest that will change your life forever."

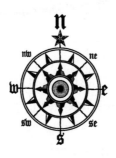

Chapter Two

Gavin awoke to the irritating sound of a rooster crowing. He stirred, stretched, and slowly opened one eye, frowning as he took in the unfamiliar surroundings. *Where am I?* he mused sleepily. *The fireplace looks familiar, and the table, and...The cottage! This is Sir Wisdom's cottage.* Abruptly, memory sharpened and he recalled the events of the night before. He sat up, and the delicious aroma of baking bread brought him wide awake.

"Did you sleep well?"

Gavin turned to see Sir Wisdom preparing the table. "Aye, sire, that I did. I slept very well."

"Excellent. Now, how about some breakfast?"

Gavin grinned. "Aye, sire, I am ready. What are we having?"

"Fresh bread and venison stew," the old man replied. "I'll have it on the table before you can reach your seat."

The words were a challenge. Gavin sprang from the pallet on the floor and leaped for the chair that he had occupied the night before, but he was not quick enough. Just as he dropped into the chair, Sir Wisdom plopped a pan of steaming bread onto the table. His friendly gray eyes were twinkling merrily. "Maybe next time, lad."

Gavin laughed.

The old man ladled a generous helping of rich brown stew into Gavin's bowl. The steam wafted around Gavin's head, and the enticing aroma reminded the youth just how hungry he was.

"So tell me about this quest that you mentioned last night," Gavin requested, as they fell to eating the delicious breakfast. "You said something about a mountain."

"Aye, the quest for Mount Thelema," Sir Wisdom replied.

"Mount Thelema? I have never heard of it."

"It's a sacred mountain far to the east. The mountain is quite rugged, and so tall that clouds obscure the peaks. There is a huge cleft in the middle so that at first observation the mountain appears as two separate mountains. The region above the clouds is never visible from the valley floor, but it is said to be a region of delights known to but few of Emmanuel's children. If you would journey to that sacred region above the clouds, you would learn of Emmanuel's plan for you."

"Mount Thelema." Gavin said the words aloud, slowly, carefully, as though awed by the sound. "Is there any significance to that name?"

"Much significance. Thelema is an ancient word meaning 'the will of the King.' In your quest for Mount Thelema, you are seeking the will of King Emmanuel."

Gavin was silent for a moment as he thought it through. "Last night you said that His Majesty has a plan for my life. Is this what you mean when you speak of the will of King Emmanuel?"

Sir Wisdom nodded as he buttered a piece of hot bread. "Exactly. If you are willing to make the journey to Mount Thelema, you will learn of Emmanuel's plan for your life."

Gavin was silent, and Sir Wisdom noticed. The keen gray eyes met Gavin's. "You do want to follow His Majesty's plan for you, do you not?"

Gavin lowered his gaze. "I think so."

"You think so? Lad, the King reveals his will to be obeyed, but not to be considered. You cannot ask His Majesty to show you his plan so that you can consider whether or not you will follow it. Emmanuel will reveal his will for you when you are ready to obey it with all your heart."

"What if I do not want to do the King's will?" Gavin asked curtly.

"Why would you not desire Emmanuel's will for you, lad? Your King can be trusted. He knows you better than you know yourself, and he loves you more than you will ever know. Finding and doing the will of King Emmanuel is the grandest accomplishment in this life, and it brings the greatest fulfillment and the sweetest rewards. You told me that you enjoyed your life as a minstrel, and yet, when you learn Emmanuel's plans for you, you will find them to be a thousand times better than your own plans."

Gavin was silent for several long moments, and Sir Wisdom waited patiently. At last, the youth gave voice to the fear that was troubling him. "What if King Emmanuel's will for me is something terrible?" he asked.

"Terrible? How could Emmanuel's will be terrible?"

"What if he wants me to be something that I just cannot be, or do something that I just cannot bear to do? Aye, Sir Wisdom, I want to serve him and I want my heart to be yielded to him. But what if his plan for me is something that would make me miserable?"

Sir Wisdom smiled and shook his head sadly. "That is a fair question, lad," he answered slowly, "and yet you would never ask that question if you understood just how much your King really loves you. Emmanuel's plan will never make you miserable—

when you find his plan for you, you will delight in doing it."

Gavin was thoughtful. "How far is this mountain?"

"The distance cannot be measured in miles or furlongs," Sir Wisdom replied. "The mountain lies far to the east, though no one can tell you just how far. You will not reach it in a day, or even in a week. Some have spent years seeking it without ever finding it. Aye, the quest will be a long one, and the obstacles will be numerous, but the rewards will be worth every step of the journey."

The youth sighed as he pondered the information that the old nobleman had just shared. "You said that some have sought the mountain and never found it," he said slowly. "How can I be certain of finding it?"

"'Ye shall seek me, and find me, when you search for me with all your heart,'" Sir Wisdom quoted. "His Majesty delights in guiding his children to the place where they find his will."

"But you told me that some have sought for years and failed to find the mountain," Gavin argued. "How can I be sure of finding it when others have failed?"

"Others have sought the mountain out of curiosity, or perhaps a sense of obligation, yet they sought it without a yielded heart. Remember, Emmanuel will not reveal his will to be considered, but to be obeyed."

Gavin was silent for a long time. Sir Wisdom waited patiently. The fire burned low on the hearth, but neither man moved.

At last, Gavin stood to his feet. "I will make the quest and seek Mount Thelema," he announced. "I seek to find the will of my King."

Sir Wisdom looked deeply into his eyes, and again Gavin felt as if the old man could see into the very depths of his soul. "But what about your heart, lad? Is it yielded to your King?"

Gavin paused before answering. "In truth, I do not know," he replied slowly, "but if it is not, will I not discover that as I make the journey?"

Later that morning, Gavin stood in the doorway to Sir Wisdom's humble cottage, arrayed in chain mail armor given him by Sir Wisdom. His heart trembled as he thought about the quest ahead of him. "But sire, how will I know which way to go? What if I lose my way? What if Argamor or his men should stop me? Sir Wisdom, can you not go with me? I don't want to go alone."

"This journey will be quite difficult, and actually perilous at times," the nobleman replied. "There are dangers of which I cannot warn you. You must beware of those who would seek to dissuade you from making the journey and those who would directly oppose you and seek to do you harm. But rest assured that King Emmanuel will guide you safely to the mountain."

Gavin attempted to adjust the strap on his Shield of Faith. "How will he guide me?"

Sir Wisdom looked at him in surprise. "With his book, of course. You do know how to use the book to choose the right path, do you not?"

"I—I'm not sure."

"Let me see your book."

Gavin reached within his doublet and withdrew the sacred book. He handed it to the old man. "Any time you face a decision or need guidance as to what path to take," Sir Wisdom instructed him, "simply open your book and turn it in the direction that you think you ought to go. The book will help you discern the way to go by glowing brightly when you turn it in the right direction."

He swung the book vigorously and in an instant it became

a sharp, glittering sword. "And of course, you will face opposition from Argamor and his forces, so you will use the book to defend yourself."

Gavin glanced up into the branches of a myrtle tree just outside the door where there perched a snow white dove of unusual beauty. "You said that the dove will guide me. How will he do that?"

"The dove knows the mind of King Emmanuel perfectly, and he will assist you in choosing the right paths. He speaks in a still, small voice, so you must be careful to pay close attention when he speaks, for his guidance is easily ignored."

"I will listen," Gavin vowed.

"And of course, the voice of the dove will always be in perfect agreement with the words of the book," Sir Wisdom continued, "for they were both given to you by Emmanuel. Follow the guidance of your book and listen for the voice of the dove and you will not go wrong."

Gavin glanced at Sir Wisdom and then looked back to the beautiful dove. "I will listen for his voice."

Sir Wisdom nodded. "Aye, my prince. Be careful that you do, for he will never lead you wrong. Obedience to his voice will guarantee success in your quest for the mountain." He paused and looked at Gavin with eyes filled with compassion. "Always remember that you can send a petition to His Majesty at any time, day or night. Your King desires success for you in this quest, and he stands ready to answer your every petition."

Shortly after being adopted into the King's family, Gavin had learned of an incredible form of communication with his gentle sovereign—whenever he desired to send a message to the King, all he had to do was write it out on a parchment, roll it up, and release it. Miraculous as it seemed, in an instant the petition would be delivered to His Majesty's throne room at the Golden City. Gavin had learned from experience that Emmanuel was eager to receive his every request.

Gavin nodded at Sir Wisdom's words. "I will make frequent use of my right as a son of the King. I will send regular petitions to His Majesty. But what about provisions for the trip? I have neither food nor money."

Sir Wisdom lifted a haversack and placed it upon Gavin's back. "This grace is provided for your journey by the lovingkindness of your King," he said.

Gavin frowned. "But you said that the quest for Mount Thelema will be quite long. The pack upon my back is rather light, and I know that it cannot contain enough provisions for such a journey."

"Your King has provided for today," the old man assured him. "Take the journey one day at a time. Tomorrow he will replenish your supply as needed."

Sir Wisdom stepped close and wrapped his arms around the youth. "Farewell, Gavin. Follow the guidance of the book, lad, and listen to the voice of the dove. Be sure to send a petition to His Majesty whenever the need arises, and you will find that his resources will meet your every need. Go in faith, my prince, and you shall have a prosperous journey. Farewell, my son. May King Emmanuel's love go with you."

"Thank you, sire. I am deeply grateful for your counsel and your help."

Gavin set out with a lively step and a merry heart. He had already forgotten the disappointments and terrors of the night before. King Emmanuel loved him and had planned a wonderful life for him, and he was going to find that plan, though the journey to Mount Thelema might be long and treacherous. A merry heart expresses itself in song, and before long Gavin was singing praises to King Emmanuel.

He was careful to follow the guidance of the book, and less than five furlongs from Sir Wisdom's cottage the path left the easy terrain of the lowlands and began to wind its way toward higher elevations. Soon he was following a narrow, winding track that wound its way along the very edge of a steep precipice. He looked down across an expanse of forest and spotted the roof of a small dwelling among the trees, and he recognized it immediately as the cottage where he had sheltered from the storm.

Thank you, Sir Wisdom, he thought gratefully. *Your advice and counsel have helped put me on the right path at last. Soon I shall know the heart and the will of my King, and I am forever grateful to you.*

The sun was warm and the trail was steep, and he soon found himself longing for a drink. When the path crossed a little stone bridge spanning a small stream, he left the path and hurried gratefully down to the stream. The water was cool to his touch and he eagerly washed his face, splashed some on his neck and arms, and then dipped up a double handful and drank deeply. A bluejay in a nearby elderberry tree scolded him vigorously and he laughed in delight. He dipped up another double handful and again drank deeply.

"Good morning to you, my young friend," a cheerful voice called, and Gavin looked up to see a tall, thin man with a mournful face and thinning hair. The man left the trail and hurried down to the stream. "Would you be so good as to share your stream with a thirsty traveler?"

Gavin laughed. "Certainly, sir. Just don't drink it all, for we may need some later."

The man laughed as he knelt at the water's edge. "Aye, and I'll save some for you." He drank noisily, wiped his mouth with the back of his hand, and then took a seat on a large boulder.

"Where are you off to, my friend? It's quite a trek through

these mountains, isn't it? The Mountains of Difficulty, folks call them, and indeed they are aptly named."

"My name is Gavin, sir, and I am on a quest to Thelema Mountain to find the will of my King."

The man's eyes registered his surprise. "Thelema Mountain, you say? And how do you propose to get there, Gavin?"

Gavin shrugged. "I intend to walk, sir. And what is your name, if I may ask?"

The man extended his hand. "I beg your pardon, Gavin, I'm forgetting my manners, I am. My name is Malcolm. I'm a cobbler by trade."

Gavin shook his hand. "I am pleased to meet you, sir." He sat down on another boulder opposite the cobbler.

"You say that you intend to walk to Mount Thelema, but just how do you intend to find it?"

"King Emmanuel's book will guide me, sir. And the dove is my guide as well."

Malcolm glanced up at the dove perched in a nearby tree and then back to Gavin. "The mountain may not be that easy to find. I say that because I myself am returning from a quest to Mount Thelema."

Gavin leaned forward eagerly. "How far is the mountain, sir? What was it like? Did you find the will of Emmanuel?"

The tall cobbler sadly shook his head. "I wish I could answer your questions, Gavin, but I'm afraid that I have no answers. Six weeks ago I set out for Mount Thelema just as eager and full of spirit as you, and just as determined to know the will of my King. But alas, you find me returning from my quest in failure. I have faced dangers and difficulties such as you cannot imagine, yet I still do not know Emmanuel's will. Mount Thelema has proven impossible to find, lad."

Gavin was stunned by the man's words. "What do you intend to do, sir?"

Malcolm shrugged. "There is nothing else to do, Gavin. I will go back home in failure." He sighed. "Allow me to give you some advice, lad, and perhaps spare you some grief. You are fresh and eager to go to the mountain—I can see it in your eyes—and that tells me that you are just starting out on your quest. May I suggest that you turn around and go back, as I am doing, rather than continuing on and meeting with defeat and discouragement, as I have done?"

He sighed again. "Lad, take it from one who knows—Mount Thelema is impossible to find."

Chapter Three

Gavin stared at the cobbler for several long moments without speaking. The man's words rang of truth and sincerity, and Gavin had no doubt that he meant every word, but the idea of turning back left an empty feeling in the depths of his soul. "I—I cannot turn back, sir, for I must know the will of my King. I must find and climb Mount Thelema."

"It's no use, lad," the cobbler said, shaking his head sadly. "I tried my best, yet could not find the mountain. In fact, there are many who say that such a mountain does not exist."

"You must beware of those who would seek to dissuade you from making the journey and those who would directly oppose you and seek to do you harm." The words of Sir Wisdom echoed in Gavin's memory like a warning bell. Perhaps Malcolm the cobbler had been sent by Argamor. He stood up. "Sir, why do you seek to dissuade me from finding Mount Thelema? Are you an emissary for Argamor?"

Malcolm's head snapped back as if Gavin had slapped him in the face. "An emissary for Argamor? Nay, lad, do not say such things! I could never serve that evil warlord!"

The cobbler's face held an expression of absolute misery and Gavin realized that his words had hurt the man deeply. *Perhaps he is telling the truth,* Gavin told himself, *and perhaps he really did try to find Mount Thelema. And yet, if he is an agent for Argamor, I must be careful not to let him set a trap for me.* "Then why do you seek to dissuade me?" he challenged.

"I—I do not seek to dissuade you, lad," Malcolm replied slowly, hesitantly. "I only seek to tell you that the journey will be harder than you can imagine, that you will face unimaginable dangers, and that the quest must end in failure. I tried, lad, yet I could not find the sacred mountain. Forgive me if I sound cruel, but neither will you. Mount Thelema, if it really exists, cannot be found by the likes of us."

Gavin frowned. "I have been told that it is a difficult quest," he told Malcolm, "but that King Emmanuel wants us to find the sacred mountain. Is that not one reason that he gave us the book?"

"The book?" The cobbler's face was blank.

"Emmanuel's book," Gavin replied, drawing his book from his doublet. "The King's book will guide us to Mount Thelema. In your quest for the mountain, sir, did you follow the book?"

"Nay, lad, I did not, for I did not know that it would guide me there," Malcolm confessed humbly, and at this, any doubts that Gavin had entertained were erased. Malcolm was telling the truth.

"Look, sir," Gavin said eagerly, opening the book and turning it so that the pages glowed, "the book will show us the way to the mountain! The pages glow when we are on the right path, but dim when we stray from the path." As he said this, he turned the book so that the pages dimmed noticeably.

Malcolm was amazed. "Lad, if that is true, we can find Mount Thelema! We can know the will of Emmanuel!" His face lit up with delight.

"Will you go with me, sir?"

"Aye, lad, that I will," the cobbler replied joyfully, "for my heart desires to know the will of my King." He stepped to the stream, dipped up a double handful of the cool water, and drank deeply. "Well, lad, shall we be off?"

"Call me Gavin, if you please, sir."

"Aye, Gavin, shall we set off for Mount Thelema? And do call me Malcolm, lad."

Gavin and Malcolm set off at a brisk pace. The trail was steep and rocky. Although Gavin was younger and perhaps more energetic than his companion, he had to walk fast to keep up, for the cobbler climbed with an enthusiasm that seemed to lend wings to his feet.

"Just ahead is a treacherous area with many rockslides," Malcolm warned a few minutes later. "We'll have to watch our step."

"Is this the way you came?" Gavin asked.

"Aye. I was coming back, you know, when we met." Malcolm sighed. "I'm sorry, Gavin, I am, that I tried to turn you from the quest. I did it in innocence, lad, for I truly believed that finding Mount Thelema was an impossibility. Would you find it in your heart to forgive me?"

"Aye, of course," Gavin responded brightly. "I will be glad to have you as a travel companion. Perhaps we can be an encouragement to each other."

"Aye, but I didn't start off too well on that one, did I now?" Malcolm commented sheepishly, and they both laughed.

"This is the place I warned you about," the cobbler said a moment later, pausing and pointing up the trail. "There are a number of rockslides, and there are areas where a rockslide could take place at any moment. Be careful."

Gavin glanced up at the mountainside above the trail. Just as Malcolm had warned, the area looked treacherous. The steep slope above the trail was littered with thousands of boulders of all sizes, many of them poised for a quick slide down the mountain. "Aye, you were right," he said to his companion, "this is a dangerous place."

"Beware!" Malcolm shouted, leaping backward and knocking Gavin down. "Rockslide!" He ran past the youth as if pursued by a pack of wolves.

Gavin leaped to his feet and dashed back down the trail. Behind him a low rumble grew louder and louder until it became a deafening roar. He spun around. Thousands of boulders of all sizes slid downward until the trail was completely obliterated. Gavin trembled at the sight. The spot where he and Malcolm had been trekking was now covered in thousands of tons of rock! "We—we could have been crushed!" he stammered.

"Ah, but praise the name of Emmanuel, we were not." Malcolm said cheerfully.

Gavin stared at him. *Quite a change from the defeated cobbler I met just a short while ago,* he thought.

A look of horror swept across Malcolm's face. "Look!" He pointed at the rockslide.

Gavin gasped in dismay. Protruding from the vast pile of rocks was a tiny human hand! Without regard for the danger of the situation, he leaped forward and fell to his knees on the rock pile. "Help me!" he cried to Malcolm. "Someone is trapped beneath the rocks!"

Working frantically, the two travelers cleared the rocks from around the hand. To their complete astonishment, they uncovered a tiny little wisp of a man less than a foot tall. Dressed in a green jerkin and brown leggings, the tiny figure lay on his back with his eyes closed. His lower face was concealed by a short, curly brown beard.

"What—what is it?" Malcolm's voice came as a nervous whisper.

"It's a person, I think," Gavin replied, also in a whisper. "But he sure is tiny, isn't he?" Bending over, he cautiously touched the tiny figure, and then picked him up, cradling him carefully in both hands.

At that moment the little man opened his eyes. He lay perfectly still in Gavin's hands, moving only his eyes as he studied his two rescuers with suspicion. Abruptly, a wide smile swept across his tiny face. "Gentlemen, I thank you!" he cried in a thin, shrill voice. "I do believe I owe my life to you."

As Malcolm and Gavin stared open-mouthed, the little man sat up. "Where's Apathy?"

"Who?" Gavin asked in a hoarse whisper. The tiny man was the most astonishing sight he had ever seen, and the youth trembled as he held him.

"Apathy," the tiny man repeated. "My friend."

Leaning over the edge of Gavin's hand, he stared down in dismay at the rockslide. "Help me," he cried. "Apathy is buried beneath the rocks!"

"There," Malcolm said, pointing to a tiny foot protruding from the rocks. Dropping to their knees, Gavin and Malcolm helped the tiny man free his friend from the rockslide. When the rocks were cleared away, Malcolm lifted the limp body and cradled it in his bony hands. Dressed in a dark blue jerkin and black leggings, the second tiny man had a long beard that reached nearly to his waist. His eyes were closed and Gavin feared that the life had been crushed out of him.

Malcolm held the lifeless body close to his ear. "I can't tell if he's breathing," he said soberly. His chin quivered and his eyes held a look of anguish.

"Let me see him," the first little man demanded. The cobbler was kneeling, so the little man scrambled up and stood upon Malcolm's thigh. Reaching up with both hands, he grabbed the cobbler's long fingers and pulled his hands down toward himself until his injured friend was at his own eye level. "Apathy, wake up!" he shouted in a tiny voice, slapping Apathy's face with a ferocity that astounded his larger companions.

Apathy opened his eyes. "Envy, what are you doing here? Where are we?"

"You and I nearly left Terrestria for good," his tiny friend told him. "We were buried under an enormous rockslide, but these kind gentlemen graciously dug us out."

"Is that true?" the tiny man in Malcolm's hands demanded, staring up at the cobbler.

Malcolm nodded. "He's telling it as it happened, little man."

"The name is Apathy," the little man responded, sitting up in Malcolm's hands. "My friend here is named Envy. And if you have indeed saved our lives, we are grateful." He suddenly grimaced and grabbed his leg. "Oh! Oh! My leg! I think it's broken!"

As Gavin and Malcolm watched in dismay, the tiny man in Malcolm's hands twisted and writhed in pain. "Can you help us?" Envy implored, wringing his tiny hands. "We must get him back to the village."

"Just show us the way," Gavin replied. "Why don't you ride on my shoulder? It will be faster." Envy nodded in agreement and scrambled up, holding tightly to the youth's doublet.

Following Envy's directions, they soon found themselves approaching a tiny village with scores of tiny houses less than three feet tall. A whitewashed sign at the side of the trail proclaimed in bold letters that were a bit difficult to read, "Welcome, traveler, to the Village of the Littlekins."

So these are Littlekins, Gavin thought.

As they hurried down a street so narrow they could barely walk side by side, Malcolm and Gavin stared in utter astonishment. *From the number of houses in this village,* Gavin thought, *there must be hundreds of these little people! This is the most amazing thing I have ever seen!*

But the biggest surprise was yet to come. As Gavin and Malcolm carried the two tiny men down the narrow street, Apathy suddenly sat up, leaped from Malcolm's hands, and shouted in a shrill voice, "We brought two big 'uns! Come and get 'em!"

At that moment, Envy leaped down from Gavin's shoulders.

Suddenly becoming aware of the clamor of angry voices, Gavin turned to see a horde of tiny townspeople rushing into the street from all directions. Many of the men carried burlap sacks that appeared to be quite heavy; the women carried coils of rope.

Gavin and Malcolm looked at each in amazement, but they were not alarmed in the least. The biggest man in the crowd was barely twelve inches tall. The angry horde of Littlekins swarmed around Gavin and the cobbler, striking and kicking at their feet and lower legs. Gavin and Malcolm laughed. The little people were attacking them in fury, but their assaults had no effect. "With one good kick I could send twenty of them flying," Malcolm told Gavin in amusement.

"Little folk, what are you doing?" Gavin cried, doing his best to hold back his laughter at the absurdity of the assault. To him, the attack of the little people seemed as frivolous as a pack of squirrels attacking a pair of lions. "We're not your enemies!"

The angry horde swelled in numbers until the street was filled with tiny villagers. Shouting and screaming in their tiny voices, they surged forward, competing with each other for the opportunity to take a swing at the two amused travelers. But their furious assault was having little effect; Gavin and his companion could hardly feel their feeble blows.

Gavin took a step backward, stumbling over some of the little people and knocking them flat, though he managed to avoid stepping on any of them. The tiny villagers responded in a blind rage, swarming forward like a colony of oversized ants and screaming in their eagerness to do him harm. The women suddenly uncoiled their ropes and began to run back and forth between the buildings, stringing multiple strands of rope across the street like a tangled spider web.

Several brave young villagers had ventured to scramble up onto the roofs of the houses. They launched themselves at Gavin and Malcolm like human missiles, some of them managing to catch hold of belts and other articles of clothing, and hung on for dear life. The two travelers brushed the tiny attackers away, doing their best not to hurt the little people.

"We are not your enemies!" Gavin called again, trying to reason with the horde of angry Littlekins. "We're just passing through on our way to Mount Thelema. Please stop! We do not wish to harm any of you."

But his words fell on deaf ears. The angry mob of Littlekins now numbered in the hundreds. The men with sacks began to upend them, scattering scores of small, round stones in all directions. The crowd surged forward, shouting and swinging and pressing against Gavin's shins until he was compelled to take several steps backward. Suddenly his boots slipped on the rocks underfoot and he found himself falling backwards. As he hit the ground, the mob shouted exultantly and swarmed over him like ants on a dead moth.

Gavin still was not alarmed as he rolled over and leaped to

his feet. If it was a fight that these Littlekins wanted, then it was a fight they were going to get! But somehow the frantic hordes of tiny villagers had managed to throw a noose around his neck, and, as he attempted to stand up, they jerked him down into the dust again. Gavin lunged upward against the tiny rope, flinging dozens of little people to the ground like so many toy dolls. He struggled to his knees, but the Littlekins pulled him to the ground again by the sheer weight of their numbers.

"Get off me!" Gavin shouted, struggling and thrashing about in a desperate attempt to free himself. "Let go of me!" He threw his arms wide, scattering Littlekins left and right. Throwing his hands to his neck, he grasped the noose about his throat and attempted to pull it open. The Littlekins swarmed over him again, shouting and kicking and hitting him.

Realizing for the first time the seriousness of the situation that he was in, Gavin pulled the book from his doublet. Instantly scores of Littlekins pounced on his sword arm and wrested the book from his grasp before he could swing it. Their combined weight flattened him to the ground. "Malcolm!" he shouted.

In desperation he looked around to see the cobbler lying prone upon the ground, bound hand and foot so tightly that he could scarcely move. As Gavin watched in dismay, nearly a hundred Littlekins surrounded Malcolm, hoisted him into the air over their heads, and carried him triumphantly down the street. Gavin shuddered, knowing that a similar fate was in store for him.

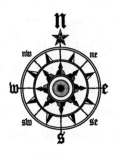

Chapter Four

"Where are we?" Malcolm groaned, rubbing his aching head and looking around in the darkness. Each time the cobbler moved his hands, the clank of heavy chains echoed in the chamber, for iron shackles were fastened to his wrists. Similar chains were upon his feet. "So where are we?" he asked again.

"I think we're in the Dungeon of Condemnation," Gavin replied soberly.

"The Dungeon of Condemnation! How did we get here?"

"We're the prisoners of the Littlekins," the youth responded bitterly. "They brought us here."

"The Littlekins? Envy and Apathy? But we saved their lives!"

"Aye," Gavin growled, "but apparently they set a trap for us. I'm beginning to think that the whole episode with the rock-slide was just a charade."

"Why, those little blackguards!" the cobbler snarled. "Just wait till I get my hands on them!"

"I don't think you'll get that chance," Gavin told him wryly. "We are locked in their dungeon, you know. I'm afraid they have us at their mercy."

Malcolm grunted as he pulled against the chains, testing

their strength. In his struggle he banged his head against the wall. "Well, this is a fine fix we're in," he growled. "Here we are, just starting out on the quest for Mount Thelema, and just like that we're rotting in a dungeon that smells like a pigsty. I still can't believe that those little rats would turn on us after what we did for them! We saved their lives!"

"Nay," Gavin argued, "I don't think so."

The cobbler stared at him. "You don't think we saved their lives? They were both buried under piles of rock! But for us, they would have perished!"

"I still think the whole thing was an elaborate ruse," Gavin told him. "I think it was a trap they set for us."

"Aye, well, we walked right into it, didn't we?" Malcolm retorted bitterly. "It seems that I was right after all—we will never make it to the mountain. Instead, we're going to rot in a dungeon run by little people less than a foot tall! Who would have thought it?"

"We're not defeated yet," Gavin replied fiercely. "We're going to leave this dungeon behind us and press on until we reach Mount Thelema and find the King's plans for us."

"Aye, just like that," his companion replied cynically. "We're just going to walk out of here as if we don't have shackles on our hands and feet! Son, wake up and look around you! We're prisoners. We're not going anywhere!"

"Are you just going to give up?"

"I don't see anything else to do. Do you have a plan?" The words were caustic and bitter.

"Nay, but Emmanuel does," Gavin responded. "He'll show us a way out of here."

Malcolm snorted. "I'm sure he will. Gavin, this is my second attempt at Mount Thelema, and again it ended in failure, just as before. Did I not tell you it would be this way?"

Gavin remained silent.

"Didn't I? Didn't I tell you that it wasn't worth trying? Didn't I tell you not to set yourself up for failure and disappointment? If we ever do get out of here—which I doubt—I'm heading straight for home. I've had enough of the quest for Mount Thelema!"

The cell door opened just then and a Littlekin walked in bearing a tray of food. Smartly dressed in a red doublet with gold braid, white leggings, and shiny black boots, he was obviously a soldier. The sword at his side was well-polished. "Good day, gentlemen," he said in a mocking tone, "I trust that you are enjoying the fine accommodations."

Malcolm snarled and grabbed for the tiny soldier, who dropped the tray and skittered out of reach just in the nick of time. "Come here, you little rat," the cobbler growled. "I'll show you some fine accommodations!"

The Littlekin grimaced in mock fear. "I'm trembling, big 'un," he said tauntingly. "Look at me—I'm trembling!" He kicked the tray within reach of his prisoners and Gavin saw to his disappointment that it contained nothing except bread and water. "Pardon me for spilling your water, Governor," the tiny guard said with mock regret. "If you hadn't been so churlish, you would have something to drink."

The cobbler curled his lip in disgust as the little soldier headed for the cell door.

"Wait!" Gavin called. "Sir, wait!"

The guard turned.

"Can you tell me why we are in here?" Gavin begged. "What have we done wrong?"

"I don't know that I'd tell you if I knew," the Littlekin responded, throwing a look of disdain in Malcolm's direction. "If you're in here, you're in here, and that's all that matters."

"But we haven't done anything wrong," the youth pleaded. "We saved the lives of two of your townspeople!"

The Littlekin soldier laughed. "Oh, I doubt that."

"But we did!" Gavin was desperate. "What—what are they going to do with us?"

"I suppose you'll stand before our magistrate, Lord Careless, for trial."

"For t-trial?" Gavin was aghast. "Trial for what?"

"Aggravating the prison guards, if nothing else," the tiny guard replied, with a snicker. "The penalty for that offense is death, you know."

"D-death?" Gavin nearly choked, and then he saw that the guard was merely having fun at his expense. "When would the trial take place?" he asked, glancing at Malcolm for support.

"How should I know?" The Littlekin shrugged. "I do know, however, that Lord Careless is out of town at the present."

"But when will he return?"

"I have no idea. Lord Careless doesn't share his travel plans with me." The guard smiled tauntingly. "Good day, gentlemen." He headed for the door.

"But how long will we be in here?"

"Don't you big 'uns ever listen? I already told that I do not know. If you're in here, you're in here, and that's all that matters."

"But can't you help us? Would you tell the town authorities that we haven't done anything wrong?"

The tiny soldier smiled. "You'll rot in here, for all I care." He hurried from the cell and to Gavin it seemed that he slammed the cell door quite a bit harder than was really necessary.

"He wasn't very helpful, was he?" Malcolm observed.

"Well, you didn't help matters any," Gavin replied, giving him a disgusted look.

"I almost caught him," the cobbler said, with a laugh. "I would have wrung his little neck and used his keys to set us free." He looked around the dismal cell. "Oh, bother, and now what are we going to do?"

⚜

The rising crescent moon threw a beam of silver light through the barred window of the dreary Dungeon of Condemnation. Gavin sighed heavily and looked over at Malcolm, who was snoring peacefully. *How can he sleep?* he thought, with a trace of resentment. *Here we are, slowly rotting in a filthy dungeon instead of making our quest for Mount Thelema. Does he not care? Has he given up completely?*

He studied the cobbler's peaceful face. *I wonder—if we were to get out tomorrow, would he go on with the quest? Or would he just turn around and go home immediately, as he has threatened more than once? If that happened, would I go on without him?* He set his jaw. *I will go on without him, if I have to. I will find Thelema and learn of Emmanuel's plans for me, no matter what it costs me!*

It had been a fortnight now, fourteen long dreary days spent in the cold, damp dungeon deep in the earth. *Will we never get out?*

Gavin sighed as he watched a large rat make its way boldly across the cell, being careful to stay just out of Gavin's reach. *That thing is bigger than any Littlekin,* the despondent youth thought grimly. *What a horrid place this is!*

If only there was some way to escape. In his mind he again searched carefully for a plan, a weakness, some way to escape the confines of the Dungeon of Condemnation. But, just as before, he came up with nothing.

"Use the Key of Faith," a quiet voice whispered.

Gavin looked around in confusion. "Who said that?"

"Use the Key of Faith to escape the dungeon." The voice was quiet, barely audible even in the silence of the prison cell, and the startled youth wasn't quite certain that he was not imagining it.

He looked around. "Who are you? Where are you?" A slight movement in the window arrested his attention and he glanced up to see the beautiful plumage of the dove gleaming like silver in the brilliant light of the moon. "Did you speak?" he asked in a whisper.

"Use the Key of Faith," the dove said, for the third time. "It is found within the pages of your book." Spreading his snowy white wings, he took to the air.

If only I had my book, Gavin thought bitterly, *but the Littlekins took it from me when they captured us.* With a deep sigh and a final glance around the darkened cell, he dropped his head to the pile of filthy straw and closed his eyes.

Malcolm was in a bad mood the next morning as he and Gavin started on their usual ration of bread and water. "I'm not sure just how much more of this I can take," he growled, to no one in particular. "I've had enough of this wretched place."

"We need to work on an escape plan," Gavin said eagerly. "There has to be some way out of here. Malcolm, there has to be!"

"Oh, don't start in on that again," the cobbler growled. "Haven't we been through this enough times? There is no way to escape from this rat hole. Would you just let it rest? Your endless chatter about an escape is almost worse than being in here!"

Gavin lapsed into silence, hurt by the bluntness of his companion's words. He took a bite of the stale, hard bread and chewed it slowly. "I just wish that the Littlekins hadn't taken my book."

Malcolm shrugged. "What difference would that make?"

"We could use it to get out of here."

"Aye," the tall cobbler replied sarcastically, "you would read of Emmanuel's plan for escape from this dungeon, would you?"

Gavin knew that Malcolm was mocking him. "You're really bitter about this, aren't you?"

"Wouldn't you be?" Malcolm angrily took a bite of bread. "Do you really think that Emmanuel cares that we are in here? We were attempting to go on a quest to learn our King's will for us—I told you it would end in failure—and look what happens! Aye, we're going to spend the rest of our lives in this stinking dungeon and our King doesn't even care."

"Don't say that," Gavin pleaded. "He does care!"

"Then why didn't he provide a way for us to escape this miserable prison?"

"He did," Gavin argued. "It's in his book."

The cobbler snorted. "Aye. There is an escape plan in your book."

"Better than that," Gavin replied. "The Key of Faith is in my book. We could use it to escape—the dove told me."

A strange look crossed the cobbler's face. "Would you say that again?"

"If I had the book, we could use the Key of Faith to escape," Gavin repeated. "It's in the book."

Malcolm the cobbler let out his breath in a long sigh of exasperation. "Then why in Terrestria did you not say something earlier? We've been in this dungeon for more than a fortnight."

"I didn't know until last night," Gavin replied evenly. "Besides, what difference would it make?"

His companion sadly shook his head and pointed upward. "Your book is on the window ledge. The Littlekins tossed it there when they threw us in here."

Gavin's mouth fell open. "Then why didn't you tell me? You're taller than me, and I never saw it."

Malcolm shrugged as he stood to his feet and reached toward the window ledge. "I didn't think it was important. You never told me about the Key of Faith." He grinned. "Come on, we're getting out of here!"

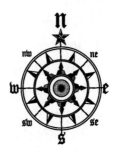

Chapter Five

The two travelers hurried up the steep slope above the Dungeon of Condemnation. Gavin paused just long enough to put the golden Key of Faith back within the pages of his precious book. "Praise the name of Emmanuel," he exulted. "He provided the key that set us free!"

"Aye, that he did," Malcolm agreed. "We serve a glorious King, do we not? It is only by his gracious provision that we are free from the dungeon. And this is one glorious day!"

Gavin stared at the man. *He's as changeable as the wind,* he told himself, *cross and anxious one moment, happy and carefree the next.*

He adjusted the pack on his back. "Can you believe that the Littlekins left our packs in the corridor of the dungeon, right where we would stumble over them?"

"Maybe Emmanuel planned it that way," Malcolm replied cheerfully.

"Well, on to Mount Thelema," Gavin said.

A cloud seemed to pass across the cobbler's face. "I think you'd do best to go on without me," he said, looking at the ground rather than at his companion. "I—I'm going to turn back and head for home. For me, the quest for Mount Thelema is over."

"Don't say that," Gavin pleaded. "His Majesty has a plan

for you, too, and you must find it! Do you not desire to find Emmanuel's will for you, to know that your life will have meaning and purpose, rather than the emptiness that comes from serving oneself?"

The cobbler sighed. "Aye, lad, I would like to know that, but perhaps it is not possible. As I told you, I have been on the quest for Mount Thelema for six long weeks, eight now, counting our time in the dungeon. To be honest, I suppose that I have just lost heart. I would like to find Mount Thelema, but I am weary of the whole matter."

"And let us not be weary in well doing: for in due season we shall reap, if we faint not."

Malcolm stared at him. "What did you say?"

"It's a quote from the King's book," Gavin told him. "Sir Wisdom showed it to me. Oh, Malcolm, go with me to the sacred mountain! Together we shall find the King's will. He will guide us and our quest shall be successful, for we have his book."

The cobbler hesitated. "I cannot bear another failure," he said quietly. "Perhaps it is best if I simply turn back now. You go on without me."

"But we are in this together," Gavin insisted. "I do not want to go on without you. How can I go to the mountain and find Emmanuel's will for me and the abundant life that he promises, when you are returning to an ordinary life that has no purpose or meaning?"

"My life will have purpose," Malcolm replied. "I will return to my life as a cobbler, making and mending shoes for people."

"Is that fulfilling?" Gavin questioned. "Does it give purpose to life?"

"I don't know that it gives purpose to life," the cobbler answered with a shrug, "but it does provide a living. It keeps food on the table and a roof over my head."

"But there is more to life than that," Gavin argued. "We were born to find and do the will of the King. There is no greater purpose in life! I don't know about you, sir, but now that I know of the existence of Mount Thelema, I cannot be satisfied until I find the King's plan for me. I will reach the mountain or die!"

"I can serve the King as a cobbler," Malcolm protested in his own defense. "And in a way, I am serving others by making the shoes that they need."

"True enough," Gavin admitted, "and yet that is not your true motivation for returning to your former life as a cobbler. When I asked you if being a cobbler gave purpose to life, you replied that it provided a living. Sir, how can you settle for less than the King's will?"

He withdrew the book from his doublet, opened it, and took out a parchment. "I will send a petition to His Majesty asking for his guidance on this quest. I will mention you—shall I tell Emmanuel that you are accompanying me, or that you are returning home in defeat?"

"Don't tell him that I am returning in defeat," the cobbler said quickly.

"Will you go with me to Mount Thelema?"

Malcolm was silent for several long moments, and Gavin could tell from his face that there was a battle raging within his heart. At last he nodded. "I will go," he said quietly. "I will not settle for less than the will of my King."

Gavin was delighted. "Then let us send a petition at once to the Golden City," he suggested, "seeking His Majesty's guidance, provision, and protection as we make the journey. It is only with his help that we will arrive safely at Mount Thelema." He spread the parchment on his knee and wrote the following message:

> "To His Majesty, King Emmanuel:
> It gives me great joy to tell you that Malcolm the cobbler is joining me on the quest for Mount Thelema. We seek to find your will for us that we might obey it. Guide us to the mountain and protect our hearts from those who would hinder us or lead us astray.
> Your son, Gavin."

Rolling the parchment tightly, he released it and watched in satisfaction as the petition shot from his hand to disappear over the crest of the mountain. "It's already in Emmanuel's hands," he told Malcolm, with delight.

"Aye, lad, it is," the cobbler agreed. "Well, shall we commence our quest?"

The two travelers started out with merry hearts and lively steps. The trail was steep, but the morning was bright and cheery with a warm, friendly sun and a gentle breeze rustling the leaves in the treetops. "I love this kind of weather," Malcolm commented.

"It's a splendid day to be traveling," Gavin agreed. "I wonder how far it is to Mount Thelema. I can't wait to see it!"

"So tell me about your life as a minstrel," the cobbler requested.

Gavin shrugged. "It was an exciting life for a time, I suppose. It gave me the chance to travel and to meet new people. We were in a different castle every night. The pay was good, and I was starting to accumulate quite a bit of money."

"So why did you quit?"

Gavin sighed. "I didn't. Sir Entertainment threw me out."

"Threw you out? Why?"

"I got sick and was losing my voice," Gavin explained simply. "Since I could no longer sing, I had no value to him. The other night during that bad storm he threw me from the coach. Like I was an old shoe or something."

Malcolm shook his head. "That's pretty rough." He eyed Gavin. "So what happened to your money?"

Gavin gritted his teeth. "It was in the coach, so I suppose that Sir Entertainment kept it. I guess you could say he stole it." He was silent as he and his companion climbed over a fallen log blocking the trail, and then said, "You know, in a way, I'm glad it happened."

Malcolm looked at him in surprise. "You're jesting."

"Nay, I'm not."

"Why do you say that?"

"Sir Wisdom says that I was serving Argamor with my life, rather than Emmanuel."

The cobbler frowned. "Were you?"

Gavin sighed. "Well, I wasn't serving the King. I pretty much did what I wanted to do. I was singing for praise and popularity and wealth, rather than for Emmanuel's glory, so I suppose you could say I was serving Argamor." He gave a sigh of contentment. "When I was thrown from the coach, I met Sir Wisdom, and he told me about Mount Thelema and how to find His Majesty's plan for my life. If I hadn't gotten sick and been thrown from the coach, I reckon I never would have heard about Mount Thelema."

His companion was thoughtful. "And if you hadn't encouraged me, I wouldn't be on the quest right now. So I guess you could say that we both can be thankful you were thrown from that coach." He laughed.

Gavin suddenly stopped in the middle of the trail as a thought struck him like an arrow from a longbow. "Do you suppose that Emmanuel planned for me to become sick and get thrown from the coach?"

Malcolm nodded. "Aye, it is quite possible." He glanced beyond Gavin and his eyes widened. "Look behind you."

Gavin turned around to find that he and Malcolm had stopped at the edge of a lofty overlook. Terrestria lay before them. The countryside far below was a peaceful vista of verdant forests, sapphire blue lakes and rivers, golden brown fields, and glistening white cities and villages. From this vantage, Terrestria looked much like a magnificent patchwork quilt. "What a view," he said quietly. "It's delightful!"

"Look at that coach," Malcolm said, pointing to a tiny landau far below. "Who do you suppose is in it, and where do you suppose they are going?"

Gavin shrugged. "How should I know?" He grinned. "But I do know this—in just a moment the coach will slow to a stop."

The cobbler laughed. "And how do you know that?"

"Look around that next bend in the road," Gavin explained, pointing. "Another coach is approaching, and the road is not wide enough for both of them at that point. One will have to back up to make room for the other."

The cobbler laughed again. "Aye, you're right." He leaned forward. "You know, from up here, it's almost as if we can see the future. Look, the coach is slowing. The driver can see the other coach now, and he's slowing, just as you said."

An idea occurred to the youth just then, and he turned to the cobbler. "You know, Emmanuel sees us in the very same way."

"What do you mean?"

"From his lofty throne, His Majesty can see our entire lives as they lie in the future. We only see one day at a time, or rather, one or two moments at a time. But he sees everything, even the future."

Malcolm nodded. "Aye, and I suppose that's one more reason to seek his will at Mount Thelema."

Both travelers turned as they heard a strange clanking sound coming from across the hillside. The noise was as if someone had put a number of cooking pots into a large bag and was shaking them about. *How strange,* Gavin thought, *but it has to be another human being.*

Moments later both saw the source of the unusual noise. A short, dark-haired man with a wide, friendly face was hiking merrily along. Battered pots and pans of every shape and size were tied to the pack on his back, clanging and banging with his every step. "A pleasant day to you, gentlemen," the friendly stranger greeted them in a cheery voice. "What a lovely day for travel, aye?"

"Indeed it is, sir," Malcolm replied. "I've never seen better. Emmanuel smiles upon us today, that is certain."

"You gentlemen certainly have a rough trek ahead of you," the stranger told them, glancing at the towering mountains behind him. "Where might you be heading?"

"We're on a quest for Mount Thelema," Gavin told him eagerly. "We seek the will of our King."

"Mount Thelema—the mountain with a cleft in the middle?" A look of alarm passed across the man's face. "Gentlemen, you might want to think twice about that. That dreadful mountain is not a place that you want to go, even for a brief visit. Nay, I would never go to Mount Thelema. Take my advice, gentlemen, and stay as far from that mountain as possible."

At these words, Gavin felt a surge of fear go through his entire being. "What do you mean, sir?" he cried. "Mount Thelema is the one place that we desire to be more than anywhere else in Terrestria! It is there that we will find the will of our great and glorious King."

"It is a place of darkness and terror," the stranger insisted.

"Why should anyone fear the sacred mountain?" Malcolm asked.

"Do you know what the peasants who live nearby call it, sir? 'Thunder Mountain,' sir. It's a place of fire and smoke, thunder and lightning, of mystery and even death. Tales are told of men climbing the mountain, never to return." The stranger shook his head vigorously. "Nay, gentlemen, you do not want to go to Thunder Mountain."

He looked from one traveler to the other. "Forgive me if I have upset you, gentlemen, but I must tell you what I know. The mountain of which you speak is the last place in all of Terrestria where I would wish to be. If you are wise, you will heed my words and return home immediately. Have a pleasant day, gentlemen."

With these words, the stranger hurried down the mountain trail, swinging his walking staff vigorously and whistling to himself. Gavin felt a cold chill sweep over him as he watched. The man's words were ominous, but was he telling the truth? Was Mount Thelema—Thunder Mountain, as he had called it—a place of peace, joy, and fulfillment, or was it in reality a place of danger?

"We need to reconsider, lad." The cobbler dropped to a seat on a large boulder beside the trail. With one hand he wiped the sweat from his brow and Gavin noticed that the hand was shaking. His face was drawn and white and his lips trembled. "Perhaps Thunder Mountain is not the place for us, after all."

"It's called Mount Thelema," Gavin retorted angrily, "not Thunder Mountain! Don't listen to the unfounded rumors that this evil man is spreading. He does not know whereof he speaks."

"But what if he does?" the cobbler asked quietly. "We dare not take that chance."

"Are you going to listen to him?" Gavin fumed. "The man was a total stranger. We have no way of knowing whether or not he was telling the truth. Perchance he was merely trying to keep us from reaching the mountain and finding the blessed will of our King."

"Why would he do that? As you said, he doesn't even know us."

"Perhaps he is an agent for Argamor," Gavin replied fiercely, "sent for that very purpose."

"Perhaps he was a friend, trying to warn us of a very real danger." Malcolm suddenly looked very old and very tired. "Do as you wish, lad, but I'm going back."

Gavin was exasperated. "Sir," he said hotly, "you change your mind quicker than a bird changes direction in flight. One moment, you're excited about the quest for the mountain, the next moment, you're ready to turn tail and run for home. You're as unstable as water!" The words were out before he could stop them.

A pained expression appeared on Malcolm's face. "Aye, lad, and I'm sorry. This time I'm changing my mind for good. I will not accompany you to Mount Thelema, and that's my final decision. Continue on without me, Gavin, and I do wish you well."

"Fine," Gavin snarled, "I'll do just that! I will continue on the quest for the mountain alone, but know this, sir—you do your King an injustice. Instead of trusting his promises, you take the word of a total stranger!"

Gavin's anger was like a steaming kettle. Once his anger boiled over, it dissipated quickly. "I'm sorry, Malcolm," he said contritely. "I didn't mean to speak so harshly."

The cobbler sat with his head down. "It doesn't matter," he said in a voice barely above a whisper. "Just go without me."

"Good-bye, Malcolm," Gavin said sadly. "I wish you the best."

"Aye, and the best to you," the cobbler replied. "May your quest be successful."

Gavin felt sick at heart as he continued up the mountain and left Malcolm sitting beside the trail. He had only known the cobbler a short while—barely more than a fortnight—but already the man had become like an older brother. *I wanted him to find Emmanuel's will also,* he told himself. *But he changed his mind so often; he never could decide what he wanted. I have to go to Mount Thelema, with or without him.* He sighed deeply. *But I will surely miss him.*

A few moments later he found that the trail made its way along the very edge of a sheer precipice. The path was narrow and a gusting wind snatched at his clothing as if determined to pull him from the safety of the trail and hurl him over the edge. Fear swept over him, paralyzing in its intensity. He had fallen from a tree as a child, and, ever afterward, had suffered from an overwhelming fear of heights. His heart was in his throat as he crept fearfully along, hugging the side of the mountain. Terrified, he paused when he came to a stunted, twisted tree growing out of the rocks. Grasping the trunk of the little tree, he stood trembling, gasping for breath and trying to quiet his pounding heart.

A petition! He would send a petition to King Emmanuel. Kneeling beside the little tree, he withdrew his book, took out a parchment, and hastily wrote an urgent plea to his King:

"My Lord, King Emmanuel:

I ask for your protection, my Lord, as I continue my quest for Mount Thelema. I am in a place of extreme danger and I am traveling alone, as Malcolm the cobbler has turned back. I beseech you, watch over me and guide me.

Your son, Gavin."

The howling wind tore at his clothing as he struggled to roll the parchment tightly. When he released the petition, the relentless wind seized it and hurled it against the side of the mountain, but the urgent message shot from the mountainside and disappeared over the crest of the ridge. Gavin gave a sigh of relief.

He stood shakily to his feet, leaning forward against the unrelenting force of the wind. At that moment he heard a faint sound, not unlike the mewing of a kitten. He paused, listening intently, but all he heard was the howl of the wind. Taking a deep breath, he started forward. The sound came again, low and far away, a thin, high-pitched wail. Gavin's heart raced. The faint sound was the desperate cry of a human being in distress!

"Halloo!" he cried, cupping his hands to his mouth and leaning into the wind. "Is someone there?"

The cry was not repeated. The only sound that came to his ears was the moaning and groaning of the wind in the crags and crevices above him.

He called again. "Is anyone there? Halloo! Are you there?"

The wind died at that moment as if pausing to take a breath.

"Help!" The cry was low and indistinct, but Gavin knew that it was the voice of a woman in distress. "Help me!"

"Where are you?" Gavin called.

"Below you! I have fallen over the cliff!"

Gavin's heart was in his throat as he knelt at the very brink of the precipice and looked over. The wind swept down from the fells at that moment, buffeting his back, seemingly determined to hurl him into the vast emptiness below. He drew back in fear. His head swam and he struggled to breathe. Below him, the side of the mountain fell away for at least three hundred feet. A fall from such a height would kill him instantly.

"Down here!" the voice called again. "I'm right below you!"

Steeling himself against the feelings of terror that threatened to overwhelm him, he forced himself to lean over for another look. The wind howled as if infuriated.

"Help me! Down here!"

Gavin's heart pounded and his breath caught in his throat. Clinging to the side of the cliff some thirty feet below him was a young woman! Her upturned face was white; her eyes were wide and filled with terror; and she trembled in every limb.

"Help me, oh, help me!" she cried.

"Hold on!" Gavin called. "I will try to help!"

What can I do? he asked himself in desperation. *I have no way to help her! I have no way to get down to her, and I have no way to bring her back up. What am I to do?*

"Help me!" the woman cried in terror. "I can't hold on much longer!"

Chapter Six

"What am I to do?" Gavin cried helplessly. "I have no way to help this poor woman, and yet she will perish if I don't do something quickly. What am I to do?"

He snatched open his book, withdrew a parchment, and hastily scrawled a desperate message:

"My King, what am I to do? Gavin."

The wind tore the petition from his hand as he released it, but it disappeared in an instant and he knew that it had safely reached the Golden City. "Hold on," he cried to the hapless woman below. "Help is on the way!"

"His Majesty has provided a way," a quiet voice said, and Gavin jumped in fright. Looking up, he saw the beautiful white plumage of the dove as he perched on the rocks above the trail.

"What am I to do?" the desperate youth cried.

"Your King has already provided a way," the dove replied in a calm, peaceful voice. "Look within your pack."

Clinging to the twisted tree with one hand, Gavin carefully removed the haversack on his back, fighting the wind for possession the entire time. With one hand he opened the pack. His probing hand touched a coil of rope and his heart leaped as he pulled it from the pack. Kneeling on the pack to keep the wind from snatching it from him, he hurriedly tied one end of the rope to the little tree and then hurled the coil into empty space below him.

"Grab onto the rope!" he called to the woman below. "It's tied securely to a tree." The rope tightened as the woman responded.

Gripping the taut rope with his right hand, he leaned over the edge of the precipice. The woman was clutching the rope with both hands. "Can you climb up the rope?" Gavin shouted.

"Nay, my strength is nearly gone."

Gavin took a deep breath. He knew what he had to do. His heart seemed to constrict with fear as he slowly backed over the edge, clinging desperately to the rope with both hands. *And to think that I was the one too afraid to even climb a tree,* he thought wryly. *Whatever am I doing here?*

Slowly, carefully, the brave youth slid down the rope one foot at a time. Within moments he had reached the woman and found to his amazement that she was a girl just about his age. Her feet were planted on a narrow ledge of rock and she gripped the rope with both hands. "Hold on for another moment or two," he encouraged her softly, positioning his feet on the ledge as he reached her. "I'm here to help you up."

She turned her face to him and he saw that her eyes were wide with fright. But he saw something else in her eyes—a raw courage that told him she would not give up easily. "I—I'm all right for the moment," she replied. "The rope is much easier to hold to than that root." With a nod of her head she indicated a small, twisted root jutting from the rocks just above her shoulder.

"I'm amazed that you didn't fall all the way to the bottom," he told her. "You would have been killed."

"Emmanuel was watching over me," she replied. She took a deep breath. "My name is Aldith. Thank you for coming to my aid."

"I'm Gavin," he replied. "I'm just thankful that I heard your cry for help. Hold on tight for a moment longer and I'll try to get you out of here." Clinging to the rope with his right hand, he reached down with his left and retrieved the end of the rope, which was some six feet below her. He passed it behind her back. "Grab this with your left hand and pass it in front of you," he instructed. "I'm going to tie it around you."

It took some doing, but with her help he managed to tie the rope securely around her waist. "You can't fall now," he told her, "but I'm not sure how to get you back up to the trail."

"I'm all right for now," she told him. "Perhaps you can go for help."

"I think you're right. Hang on, and I'll be back as quickly as possible." Hand over hand, he climbed the rope back to the top of the precipice, though the rope was taut and it was the most difficult thing he had ever done. When he reached the edge and managed to swing one foot up, he knew he was going to make it. Moments later, he lay gasping on the trail.

Aldith is still down there, he told himself, after a moment's rest. *I have to get help.*

"I'll be back as quickly as possible," he shouted down to the girl, and his voice echoed across the emptiness of the chasm below him.

"I'll just wait here," Aldith called, and Gavin had to laugh. Even in this life-threatening situation, the girl had a sense of humor.

Forgetting his fear of heights, Gavin dashed frantically down the narrow trail. *Where will I go for help?* he asked himself. *I can't go to the Littlekins, and as far as I know, there's no one else for miles. What shall I do?*

Moments later he rounded a bend in the trail and saw to his amazement that Malcolm was still sitting upon the boulder where he had left him. The cobbler was silent and forlorn, and didn't even look up at his approach. "Malcolm, am I glad to see you!" Gavin said, shouting in his exuberance and grabbing the man by the shoulders. "I need your help!"

Malcolm still didn't look up. "I'm not going with you, Gavin," he stated flatly. "And that's final. I will not make another quest for Mount Thelema."

"I need your help," Gavin exclaimed again. "A young woman has fallen over the cliff and is in danger of falling to her death! I need your help to pull her to safety."

The cobbler slowly raised his eyes, searched Gavin's face for a moment, and then dropped his gaze. "I can't go with you, lad," he said slowly, sadly, as he shook his head. "I just can't."

Gavin was nearly beside himself. "I can't do it alone," he pleaded. "This woman will die unless we can pull her to safety!"

There was an abrupt change in Malcolm's eyes and a puzzled look appeared on his face. "Woman? What woman?"

"A woman has fallen over the cliff and may fall to her death," Gavin repeated urgently. "I need your help to pull her to safety. Malcolm, I can't do it alone!"

"Aye, of course I'll help you," Malcolm said, rising to his feet. "What are we waiting for, lad?"

Gavin dashed up the steep mountain trail with Malcolm right on his heels. When they reached the place where Aldith had fallen, Gavin dropped to his knees, gripped the rope, and leaned over. "I brought help!" he shouted. "We'll pull you up in a moment. Are you all right?"

"I'm fine," the girl shouted back. "But I am getting very tired."

Malcolm knelt and peered over the edge. His face turned white when he saw Aldith's predicament. "Oh, my!" He looked at Gavin. "Whatever are we going to do?"

"Together we can pull her up," Gavin replied matter-of-factly, hoping that Malcolm in his timidity would not question the statement. "I couldn't do it by myself, but together we can do it."

The cobbler's face showed that he was not at all certain about the matter, but he nodded and said, "All right. Let's do it." He took a firm stance and gripped the rope with both hands. Gavin took a position across from him and gripped the rope.

"We're ready to pull you up," Gavin called to Aldith. "Climb as we pull." He glanced at Malcolm. "Ready? Pull!"

Hand over hand, the two men slowly pulled on the rope, drawing the hapless girl up toward them. As the rope lifted her weight, Aldith was able to help by climbing the face of the cliff. Within moments her face appeared at the edge of the precipice and the two men pulled her to safety. Gavin heaved a tremendous sigh of relief when she was safely back on the trail.

Aldith panted as if struggling for breath. Clutching her heart, she breathed, "Thank you, oh, thank you! You have saved my life."

"We were glad to do it," Gavin replied, kneeling on the trail and pulling at the knots that bound her. "Emmanuel sent us, I am sure. We are thankful that we were able—"

The girl looked up at that moment, and Gavin paused abruptly, struck dumb by the beauty of the girl he had just rescued. Aldith's face and hands were dirty and her clothing was rumpled and scraped, to be sure, but beneath the dirt and grime were delicate features that were breathtakingly lovely.

Long, brown hair framed a pleasant face with large, expressive eyes and a lovely mouth with lips like rose petals. The girl was dressed in the simple clothing of a peasant, but there was a regal beauty about her person that suggested royalty. Aldith smiled, revealing lovely white teeth, and Gavin felt as if his heart had stopped.

"We were—we were..." Gavin paused, dumbfounded, forgetting what he was trying to say. He stood, open-mouthed, staring at the lovely young woman before him. It took him a moment to recover. "Are you—are you all right?"

Aldith looked at her dirty hands and then glanced down at her disheveled clothing. "Aye," she replied quietly, "Emmanuel has indeed watched over me. I am fine."

"How did you come to fall over the edge, lass?" Malcolm asked. "The trail is narrow, to be sure, but how did you fall?"

"I was careless in my walk, I suppose," she replied thoughtfully, as if considering the same question for herself. "I remember seeing an eagle soaring above the valley, and I was watching it, and suddenly...well, I found myself falling over the edge."

"Aldith, this is Malcolm," Gavin said, never taking his eyes from Aldith's face. "He and I were traveling companions for awhile."

"I am pleased to make your acquaintance, sir," the girl replied, with a slight curtsy. "Thank you, sir, for saving my life." She looked at Gavin. "And thank you, sir, as well. I owe my life to both of you."

"Where are you going, lass?" the cobbler asked. "The trail is treacherous, and yet it appears that you are traveling alone—is that correct?"

Aldith nodded. "Aye, sir, I am on a quest to Mount Thelema to discover the will of my King."

Gavin's heart leaped. "Mount Thelema! That's where we are

going—well, Malcolm and I were going. Would you care to travel with us...uh, with me?"

The girl looked from Gavin to Malcolm and back again. "I would be honored to travel with you." She laughed, and her voice had the sweet tone of a silver bell. "Hopefully, you will not have to rescue me from any more precipices. I think I have learned my lesson."

Gavin laughed with her, and his heart pounded furiously. *Aldith is going with us!* he thought jubilantly. *What a lovely travel companion she will be!*

Aldith failed to see the excitement that displayed itself in Gavin's eyes, for she was entertaining thoughts of her own. "Will you both go with me?" she asked, looking from one companion to the other.

Malcolm hung his head. "Nay, my dear young lady, for I am not going to Mount Thelema. You and Gavin will have to go without me."

"Not going to Mount Thelema?" Aldith's expression showed her amazement. "But then perhaps you have already been, sir, and already know the will of King Emmanuel?"

Malcolm was silent, but Gavin could tell that the cobbler was embarrassed by Aldith's question. "Malcolm and I were on the quest for Mount Thelema," Gavin told her, "but he chose to return home."

"Oh." The girl's face betrayed her bewilderment, but she said no more.

Gavin turned to Malcolm. "Will you not reconsider, sir, now that there are three of us? We can travel together and be a source of strength and encouragement to each other. As the King's own book says, sir, 'A threefold cord is not quickly broken.' Go with us, sir, and we shall discover Mount Thelema together."

Malcolm smiled sadly. "Thank you for asking, Gavin, but my

mind is made up. I will not undertake another quest for the mountain."

"Do you not desire the King's will, sir?" The question came from Aldith, direct and abrupt, but without a hint of condemnation or judging.

"Aye," Malcolm stammered, "but—" He sighed heavily. "I—I just can't..." He fell silent, glancing at Gavin as if asking for help.

"We have been told that Mount Thelema is a place of danger and dread," Gavin explained to Aldith, "and Malcolm has believed these tales, though I think they are unfounded and untrue. Malcolm was traveling with me to the sacred mountain, but he has turned back and is now returning home."

"But he is here now," the girl said, with some confusion.

"Aye," the cobbler said quietly, "but only because Gavin told me that you were in danger."

"He came back to help rescue you," Gavin told her, gazing in wonder at the lovely eyes. "I want him to continue with us on the quest for Mount Thelema, but he is determined to go back home." He sighed. "I want him to find Emmanuel's plan for him, just as I intend to do."

Malcolm shook his head. "Aye, lad, and yet you know that is something I just cannot do."

An idea struck Gavin just then and he turned to the cobbler, hardly able to contain his excitement. "What if King Emmanuel himself were to show you the way to the sacred mountain?" he asked. "Would you go then?"

"Aye, that I would," the man answered. "I do desire His Majesty's will, Gavin. It's just that—well, I have tried and failed. I will not try again, for I will not fail again."

"But you would go if the King himself would guide you?" Gavin prompted.

"Aye, for then we should be assured of success," Malcolm responded. "And then I would know for certain that a visit to the mountain is what the King has planned for me."

Gavin opened his book. "Remember, sir, that the King himself will guide us, for he has given us his book! Look, sir, this trail will lead us to Mount Thelema, for the book glows brightly when it faces in the direction of the trail. And see, when I turn the book in another direction, the pages dim, for this is not the right direction."

The cobbler leaned forward eagerly. "Aye, lad, I should have remembered. If the King's book will guide us to the mountain, then I will go on this quest, for I do desire to know Emmanuel's will."

Gavin was overjoyed. "Then let us be off at once," he cried, "for I am certain that we still have a long way to go." In his excitement, he failed to see a dark, hideous creature lurking on the rocks above him, eagerly listening to every word.

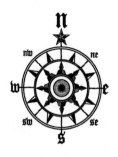

Chapter Seven

Gavin, Aldith, and Malcolm set off at a brisk pace, eagerly striding up the trail in spite of the steepness of the incline. The day was bright and sunny and the brilliant blue sky overhead was laced with an occasional fleecy cloud. "Perfect weather for a journey, is it not?" Malcolm remarked cheerfully.

"Aye, that it is," Gavin agreed. "And the journey is made sweeter by your company, sir." He glanced at Aldith and took a deep breath. "And by yours, too, of course."

The path grew steeper and more rugged. Before long the trail had disappeared entirely and the three travelers found themselves scrambling over huge boulders and climbing sheer rock faces. The cliffs were rough and porous and offered excellent handholds, but the going was slow and laborious and most frightening. From time to time Gavin checked the book to make sure that they were still traveling in the right direction.

Gavin watched Malcolm's face, trying to determine if the difficulties of the journey were affecting him, but the cobbler seemed cheerful and almost eager as they faced each obstacle. Aldith seemed to have recovered from her ordeal and she climbed as readily as the two men.

"Look!" Aldith cried, as she and her two companions crested

a ridge and realized that they had reached the summit of the mountain. The three travelers stood in awe as they gazed across a breathtaking panorama of purple mountains and verdant forests, sapphire lakes, tiny villages, and lush farms. A vast region of Terrestria was visible from this vantage, and the view was overwhelming in its beauty.

"It's as if we can see all of Terrestria from here," Gavin said softly, as he came up beside Aldith.

"And my father owns it all," she replied.

"Aye, we serve a mighty King," Malcolm commented. "What we are seeing is actually a tiny portion of Terrestria, yet Emmanuel created it all by simply speaking it into existence."

"Well, shall we take a short rest and then continue?" Gavin suggested. "The going ought to be quite a bit easier from now on."

"At least for awhile," Malcolm said wryly. "I see other mountains before us, and we all know how we're going to cross those."

Aldith laughed. "I, for one, am ready for a rest." She sank onto a large, flat boulder and closed her eyes. "Listen," she told the others. "It sounds as if the wind is singing to us!"

After a brief rest they continued on their quest. The trail wound its way down the side of the mountain for a time, but then soon began to climb again. Malcolm paused when he came to a fork in the path. "Which trail do we follow?" he asked. "The one to the left is wide and fairly smooth, but the one to the right is narrow and rather rocky."

"Let's take the one to the left," Aldith suggested. "Look—it goes downhill, while the other goes uphill. The path to the left will be easier."

Malcolm nodded. "Your suggestion makes sense, lass. We'll take the trail to the left."

"Wait!" Gavin protested, and his companions looked at him

in surprise. "The easiest path is not necessarily the right one. Does not the King's book say that the road to destruction is broad, but the road to life is narrow?" He pulled his book from within his doublet. "Should we not at least consult the book?" He opened the book and studied the pages. "Aye, just as I thought," he announced, but there was not a trace of arrogance in his voice. "The book says to take the narrow trail."

Aldith had watched the entire process and saw for herself that the pages of the book glowed brightly when the volume was turned to the right, but dimmed noticeably when turned to the left. "It actually does guide you, doesn't it?" she remarked in astonishment. "The book is actually showing you which trail to follow."

Gavin nodded. "Sir Wisdom told me that it would, and it does."

Malcolm spoke up. "So if we follow the book, we take the narrow trail to the right."

At midday the travelers paused beside a swift, rock-lined stream and refreshed themselves with a cool drink. "It's about time to eat," Aldith suggested, turning in a slow circle as she took in the beauty of the little glen. "Why don't we have lunch right here? We won't find a prettier spot than this."

The others agreed and took their haversacks from their backs. Gavin frowned as he watched Malcolm open his pack. "Where did you get your pack?" he asked. "It is exactly like mine."

The cobbler opened his pack and pointed to the underside of the flap. "Does yours say 'faithfulness' right here? Mine does."

Gavin opened his pack and looked. "It does," he replied, with some surprise. "I hadn't seen that." He frowned in bewilderment. "But where did you get your pack?"

"It was given to me by an old man when I first set out on the quest for Mount Thelema," the cobbler said slowly, thoughtfully. "He said it was a gift from King Emmanuel, provision for my journey. In truth, I had opened it, but had never used it."

"I received mine from a nobleman named Sir Wisdom," Gavin replied, "and he told me the very same thing."

"That is exactly how I received mine," Aldith said, and her eyes were shining with excitement. "King Emmanuel has provided for our journey."

"We rescued you with a rope from my pack," Gavin told her. "His Majesty provided for your rescue before the incident even happened."

"I have no rope in my pack," Malcolm told them, rummaging through the contents of his own haversack. "All I find is food."

Gavin nodded. "Well, shall we eat?" After sending a brief petition of thanks to the King, the three travelers enjoyed a simple meal of parched corn, bread, and cheese.

The afternoon shadows were growing long as Aldith, Gavin, and Malcolm hiked wearily across a narrow, rocky ridge. Boulders as big as houses towered over them, intimidating them with their sheer size. The wind howled as it swept down upon them, snatching at their clothes and nipping at their hands and faces. "Night is almost upon us, lad," Malcolm observed. "Perhaps we should stop and make camp for the night."

Gavin stopped in the middle of the trail and looked around. "Where would you suggest, Malcolm? This ridge is pretty exposed and we have no tents for protection."

"Let's make camp in the lee of that boulder," Malcolm suggested, pointing. "It would at least block some of the wind."

"We'd do better up in that wooded area just ahead," Gavin replied. "We'd be more protected."

"I'm too tired to go another step," Aldith declared, dropping to a seat on a fallen log. "I'll rest while you two discuss it."

"I still think we should stay under the edge of that boulder," the cobbler replied. "It would offer a bit of protection from the rain."

Gavin shrugged. "As you wish, sir." He glanced again at the dark forest. "I'll at least gather some branches and build a lean-to against the boulder. Why don't you stay with Aldith? I'll be right back."

"I wish we had some way to build a fire to keep wild animals away," Aldith said wistfully, glancing about as if expecting monsters to sweep down upon them. "There's plenty of firewood, but no way to start a fire."

Thunder rumbled in the distance and Malcolm glanced skyward. "This doesn't look too good," he said quietly. "We may have rain before long." High overhead, dark clouds came sweeping in from the north, boiling and swirling angrily.

"I'll hurry." Dropping his pack, Gavin turned and sprinted up the trail. Just as he entered the forest, a light rain began to fall. The forest was dark and gloomy, and the trail was indistinct and hard to follow. *I won't venture in far,* Gavin told himself, *or I shall easily get lost. I can hardly see the trail!*

Spotting a slope littered with brush and dead branches, he hurried toward it. As he bent down to pick up the first branch, he caught a glimpse of a stone wall through the tangle of trees. Intrigued, he ran up the slope and then stopped in astonishment. Perched on the side of the mountain less than ten yards above the trail was a small log cabin! The stonework that he had spotted was the chimney of the little dwelling.

Holding his breath in anticipation, he skirted the cabin and approached the door. A brass plate on the door caught his attention and he leaned close to make out the letters in the dying light. His heart leaped as he read aloud, "Welcome, weary traveler. Enter and take your rest. This haven is provided by the grace of your King, Emmanuel." He felt like shouting.

Without taking the time to enter the little cabin, Gavin raced down the trail. "You'll never guess what I just found!" he shouted to Malcolm and Aldith as he neared the boulder where they had intended to make camp. "I found a cabin!"

"A cabin?" Malcolm echoed. "I wonder who owns it?"

"It's King Emmanuel's!" Gavin exclaimed. "There's a plaque on the door telling us that we can use it."

Aldith gave a cry of delight. "How far?"

"Less than three hundred yards from here. It's right beside the trail."

"Then let's hurry and get in out of this rain," Malcolm replied, for the rain was beginning to fall in earnest. "If we stay here we'll be soaked."

Moments later the three travelers rushed up on the porch of the little cabin, delighted to find shelter from the rain. Gavin tried the door and found it unlocked.

He threw open the door and all three were amazed to see the warm yellow glow of a lamp. As they gratefully entered the dwelling, they found a cheerful fire crackling on the hearth and a small table with three place settings. Gavin stared at the furnishings and then turned to Malcolm. "It's almost as if we were expected," he said in a hoarse whisper, "but no one could possibly have known that we were coming! No one."

Malcolm was thoughtful. "King Emmanuel knew," he replied quietly.

"There are two small bed chambers with bunks," Aldith

informed them, as she returned from a doorway where she had darted. "I'll take the chamber on the left; you two can have the one on the right."

"As you wish," Malcolm replied cheerfully. "I'd be happy to sleep on the floor, just as long as we're out of the rain."

"Well, tonight you can sleep in a real bed," she said with a laugh. "Isn't this great?" She looked around the room, noticing the table and the service for three. "There are three place settings," she said in a timid voice, as if the idea worried her. "Who could possibly have known that we were coming?"

"I was wondering the same thing," Gavin told her. "Malcolm thinks that this is Emmanuel's provision for us, and I think that perhaps he's right."

Malcolm had set his haversack on the table and was in the process of opening it. "Well, let's get supper, shall we?"

Gavin and Aldith joined him and produced food from their own packs. "Well, we'll eat tonight, but not tomorrow," Aldith said wistfully. "I have food for tonight only and then my pack is empty."

"Likewise," Gavin told her. "My pack is also empty."

Within minutes they were enjoying a meal of dried fruit, barley bread, and jerked venison. Malcolm studied the little cabin as they ate, and his face showed that he was bewildered. Gavin noticed. "What are you thinking about?"

"How do you suppose this cabin got here?" Malcolm asked, looking from Aldith to Gavin as he bit into a large chunk of the dark bread.

Gavin shrugged. "His Majesty commissioned a crew to build it," he replied. "Why do you find that so unusual?"

"But it was built at the exact spot where we needed it the most. There are three place settings at this table, as if someone were expecting three guests tonight. There are three of us."

BOOK ONE: TALES FROM TERRESTRIA

"It's as if someone knew that we were coming," Aldith finished.

The cobbler nodded. "And then today when you needed a rope to rescue Aldith, there was one in your pack. I don't have one in my pack, and neither does Aldith. What does that tell you?"

"Someone knows about our quest for the sacred mountain and is doing everything to make sure that we get there," Gavin suggested.

"Exactly," the cobbler agreed. "And we all know who that someone is—our King. I'm anxious to see what's going to happen in the next few days. If Emmanuel has this journey planned this well and knows our needs so intimately, imagine what plans he has for our lives."

Gavin was stunned by the thought. "Then Emmanuel's will for me ought to be absolutely perfect."

"I'm sure of it," Malcolm replied. "Oh, how could I have ever doubted him? He knows us, and he has provided just what we need for this journey. Can I trust him with my life? Can I trust his plans for me? I'm beginning to think that I can."

"But we have no food for tomorrow," Aldith pointed out.

"Tomorrow is another day," Malcolm told her. "Let's take this quest one day at a time."

"Take therefore no thought for the morrow," Gavin quoted, "for the morrow shall take thought for itself."

Gavin and Malcolm were awakened the next morning by a shriek from Aldith. They rushed out of the bed chamber to find the girl standing beside the table with her haversack opened upon it. "One of you had food," she accused. "You put food in my pack."

Malcolm glanced at Gavin and then replied, "Neither of us has any food, Aldith. We finished everything last night."

Her eyes grew wide. "Then someone entered our cabin last night," she said, and she trembled at the idea. "There is food in my pack! Look! Someone has put food in my pack."

Malcolm shook his head. "No one entered the cabin," he assured her.

Her eyes grew even wider. "Are you saying that my pack is enchanted?"

"Nay, not at all."

"Then where did the food come from?"

Gavin hefted his own haversack from beside the hearth. "My pack is heavy as well," he observed, "and unless I miss my guess, it is filled with food for the day's journey."

Malcolm grinned broadly. "What were we talking about last night? Our King knows about this quest for Mount Thelema; he knows our needs; and he has provided for us. Why don't we thank him for his provision and then partake? I, for one, am hungry."

At these words, Aldith and Gavin abruptly sat down at the table and the meal began.

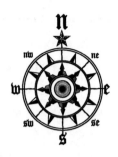

Chapter Eight

The trek through the Mountains of Difficulty took nearly a week. On most days the three travelers faced gale force winds that battered them incessantly from morning till night. Often they faced extreme danger when the trail wound its way along precipices almost too narrow for a human to pass. Rockslides were commonplace, and more than once they were nearly swept to their deaths when thousands of tons of rock abruptly let loose and thundered into the mighty chasms below, obliterating the trail.

Often they heard wolves howling in the crags and crevices above them, reminding them that they were not alone in the mountains. Aldith shuddered with terror each and every time it happened. The trials and difficulties were numerous and more difficult than they had imagined, to say nothing of the rigors of the arduous climb.

"When will we ever get out of these dreadful mountains?" Aldith wondered aloud, as they struggled to climb over one of the many rockslides. "It seems that there is no end to this trail—we're always climbing, climbing, climbing."

Gavin reached down to help her. "I think we're almost out of the mountains. King Emmanuel knows our needs and he has provided for us every step of the way."

She nodded wearily. "I know," she replied with an apologetic smile. "I don't mean to complain, and yet I am so weary of climbing."

A wolf howled just then in the crags and crevices above them and Aldith shuddered. "As if the trek through the mountains isn't bad enough, we also have the wolves to keep us company." She smiled again. "Forgive me for complaining."

At last, mid-morning on the seventh day of the quest, the trail wound its way down out of the mountains and entered a wide, peaceful valley, green with lush grass and tall, stately trees. "Quite a change from the mountains, aye?" Aldith commented. "I wouldn't mind if I never see a mountain again! And the constant howling of those wolves—it makes me shudder to even think about it." As if to prove the veracity of her words, at that moment, she shuddered.

"Wolves live in the valleys, too," Gavin replied, teasing her.

She shuddered again. "Please don't remind me."

"The journey through the Mountains of Difficulty will leave its mark on our memories, of that I am certain," Malcolm remarked. "We faced more dangers and difficulties than we had imagined, and in truth, the trek was hard. But it is in these very difficulties that I have learned many valuable lessons."

Gavin studied him. "What lessons?"

"I have learned that I can trust my King," the cobbler replied simply. "I have seen his guidance when the way was all but impossible to find; I have seen his protection when danger threatened, and I have seen his faithful provision for our every need. Each and every night of our journey through the mountains we found a cabin at just the right location. My haversack holds just enough provisions for today, yet I need not fear tomorrow, for I have seen his provision day after day, one day at a time. Aye, my young friends, I have learned to trust my King."

He smiled in triumph. "I now know that I can trust my King to take us through all the way to Mount Thelema. We shall indeed find the sacred mountain, and we shall soon know the will of our King."

At that moment the attention of the three travelers was arrested by the sound of carriage wheels, and they turned as one to see a large, stately coach bearing down upon them at high speed. "Would you look at that!" Gavin exclaimed, as they hurried to the side of the road to avoid being run down. "That is the most elegant coach I have ever seen."

The carriage swept past them in a cloud of dust. "Wouldn't that be wonderful to travel in comfort and style," Aldith remarked, looking wistfully at the speeding coach. "Imagine how much faster we would get to our destination, and imagine how much easier it would be than walking."

"Perhaps Emmanuel did not plan for us to ride in style and comfort," Gavin replied.

"Oh, I know," Aldith said quickly, "and I'm not complaining." She flashed him a grin. "But you have to admit, riding in that coach would be much more comfortable than walking."

The coach abruptly came to a stop some hundred yards beyond them. The driver, a small man in elegant gray livery, dismounted and walked back toward them. "I wonder what this is all about," Malcolm muttered.

The driver bowed as he approached. "My lady would like a word with you," he said politely, "if you please."

"Certainly," Malcolm replied pleasantly. "How may we help?"

"Come with me, if you please," the driver responded, beckoning with his hand and then striding briskly toward the waiting coach. Aldith, Malcolm, and Gavin followed warily.

Upon reaching the coach, the driver opened the door and stood to one side. "If you please, my lady is waiting."

Gavin paused beside the coach and took a quick look inside. The furnishings and appointments of the coach were more luxurious than anything he had ever seen. Thick, rich carpeting, plush upholstery, gleaming gold fittings—the interior of the carriage was designed for elegance and comfort, and no expense had been spared.

The carriage was empty save for a plump, richly dressed woman who appeared to be in her early thirties. The woman's face was pale and pasty, and her dark, well-coiffed hair was piled high upon her head in the manner of women of wealth. Her clothing was rich and costly, all satins and silks and brocades, and her presence sparkled with golden jewelry. "Please forgive the intrusion, my good people," the woman called in a polite but stiff voice, as she caught sight of the trio, "but would one of you be so good as to step into the carriage? I must have a word with you."

Gavin was closest, so he stepped up into the elegant carriage. "Please, my good man, be seated," the woman requested.

Gavin sat gingerly on a velvet cushion of the deepest purple.

"A thousand pardons, my good fellow, but it seems that my driver and I have lost our way and require some directions. Would you be so kind as to help us?"

"Certainly," Gavin replied. "I will help if I can." He glanced uneasily through the open door at Malcolm, but the cobbler seemed relaxed as he stood beside the coach.

"We are on a journey to a sacred mountain known as Mount Thelema," the rich woman told him. "We have somehow lost our way and are not at all certain that we are on the right road." She leaned forward eagerly. "Have you heard of Mount Thelema? Are we on the right road?"

Gavin was taken aback at the mention of Mount Thelema. "Indeed, you are on the right road, my lady," he assured her.

She looked him over from head to toe as if trying to decide whether or not to trust him. She glanced at her driver and then back to Gavin. "Are you certain, sir?"

"Aye, we are certain, my lady," Gavin replied evenly. "At this very moment we also are on a quest for Mount Thelema."

The woman's face registered her surprise. "Indeed. What a coincidence." Her gaze swept over the three travelers and then lingered on Gavin. "But how do you know that this is the way?"

Gavin withdrew his book and opened it. "The King's book is guiding us, my lady. Look—the pages are glowing brightly, indicating that this is the right way to Mount Thelema. Should I turn the book to one side, like this—"

"You have convinced me," she replied, interrupting him. "I thank you for your time."

Gavin stood and bowed. "I was glad to be of assistance, my lady. Have a safe and prosperous journey."

"May I wish you and your companions the same, sir," the woman replied. "Have a pleasant day."

Gavin stepped down from the carriage and the driver closed the door. Moments later, the elegant carriage was making its way across the plain at a rapid pace. Aldith watched it with wistful eyes. "Well, you got to sit in it," she told Gavin, with a teasing smile. "Do you feel like nobility?"

He laughed. "It was luxurious, I will admit."

"The coach is stopping again," Malcolm observed. "I wonder what she wants now."

As he spoke, the coach again rumbled to a stop. Just as before, the driver climbed down and hurried back to them. He bowed as he approached. "If you please," he said politely, "my lady would like a word with you again."

"Certainly," Malcolm replied pleasantly. Aldith, Malcolm, and Gavin followed the man back to the coach.

Upon reaching the coach, the driver again opened the door and stood to one side. "If you please, my lady is waiting."

"Forgive my intrusion again, my good people," the occupant of the coach said, "but would you be so good as to step inside?"

Malcolm glanced at his companions, shrugged, and then stepped up inside the carriage. Gavin and Aldith followed.

"Be seated, if you please, and please forgive the intrusion." The woman watched as they took seats upon the plush cushions. "I am Lady Katherine, Countess of Windsoar. My late husband was the Earl of Windsoar." She looked from one to another as if to determine that they were properly impressed. She hesitated, and then continued. "I was thinking—since I am traveling to Mount Thelema, and since you are traveling to the same destination, would it not make sense to travel together? You have the book, and I have the carriage, and perhaps we can be of mutual benefit to each other."

She paused, lifted her chin, and said, "I am inviting you to travel in my carriage to Mount Thelema."

At these words, a look of sheer delight spread across Aldith's face. "We would love to travel with you!" she blurted. "Wouldn't we, gentlemen?"

Gavin and Malcolm looked at each other. "I see no reason why we could not," Malcolm replied, "providing that my friend Gavin is agreed."

Aldith looked pleadingly at Gavin.

Gavin shrugged. "It would make the journey faster and easier," he agreed. "We will reach Mount Thelema much sooner this way."

"Then it is settled," Lady Katherine said, with a tilt of her head. "Let us be on our way."

The door closed with a slight click. Moments later, the three travelers settled into the plush cushions as the coach started forward. Aldith wore an expression of rapture.

Lady Katherine studied Malcolm for several moments. "Of what trade are you, sir?"

"I am a cobbler, my lady. My name is Malcolm."

"A cobbler. I see." She turned to Gavin. "And you, sir?"

"I am a minstrel, my lady, or was until recently. My name is Gavin. And this lady is Aldith."

"A minstrel? Indeed." The lady seemed impressed with this piece of information. "Perhaps you would do us the honor of regaling us in song at the next castle. Surely you could borrow—what do you call that instrument with all the strings? The one with the long neck."

"A lute, my lady?"

"Aye. Surely you can borrow a lute from one of the musicians."

Gavin nodded. "I would be honored to play for you, my lady."

For several moments the four occupants of the coach rode in silence. "May I ask you something, my lady?" Gavin requested. "How did you make it through the Mountains of Difficulty with this coach? In many places the trail was almost too steep and narrow for a human on foot. There is no way that you could have taken the coach through."

"The Mountains of Difficulty?" Lady Katherine responded. "I did not travel through any Mountains of Difficulty."

"Then how did you get to this point?" Gavin asked.

"The path to Mount Thelema is not necessarily the same for everyone," Malcolm reminded him. "King Emmanuel's plans for each of his children vary greatly, of that I am sure."

Gavin nodded. "That makes sense, sir." He turned to Lady Katherine. "We wish to thank you for allowing us to ride with you."

She nodded stiffly. "Thank you for using your book to show us the way."

Moments later the rumble of thunder sounded in the distance. "It sounds like we might be in for a storm," Malcolm commented.

"Aren't you glad we're riding now, instead of walking?" Aldith said teasingly to Gavin. "I don't know about you, but I'd rather not walk through a thunderstorm."

The thunder rumbled again, louder and closer this time. Gavin looked out the coach window. The carriage was passing through a series of rolling hills, but the sky above was bright and sunny. "I see no sign of a thunderstorm," he told the others. "The sky is clear and sunny."

At that moment the coach came to an abrupt stop. Lady Katherine leaned forward with a look of annoyance on her face. "What does Matthew think he's doing?" she fumed. "He knows not to stop unless I order it."

The coach door opened just then. "Begging your pardon, my lady," the driver said, poking his head in the doorway, "but there is a rockslide ahead. We'll have to turn back."

"A rockslide?" the woman echoed, in a tone that suggested that she thought the slide was her driver's fault. "Well, drive around it."

Matthew shook his head. "Begging your pardon, my lady, but that's quite impossible. The road is completely impassable. The coach would never make it over the rocks. We'll have to back up."

Lady Katherine's face showed her impatience with the situation. "Very well. But get us on our way as swiftly as possible."

The driver nodded. "Aye, my lady."

Another rumble of thunder resounded throughout the valley, very close and threatening, but this time the sound came from behind the carriage. Matthew turned his head and took one look, and his face fell. "My lady, there's a rockslide behind us now. The coach is boxed in."

Lady Katherine was furious. "Well, don't just stand there! Do something! Clear the roadway and get us moving again."

Matthew timidly shook his head. "Begging pardon, my lady, but that would be impossible. It would take several men and a team of mules at least a day or two to clear this many boulders from the way."

The woman snorted in disgust. "So it wasn't thunder that we heard." She glared at her driver. "Could the horses cross the rockslide?"

Matthew paused. "Aye, with caution."

"Then unhitch the horses and take them across the rocks. The four of us will continue on horseback, though I detest traveling that way. Go into one of the villages and hire men to help you clear the road. Once the road is open, buy more horses and catch up with us again."

The driver nodded. "Aye, my lady. Right away, my lady." He looked at Malcolm. "Will you help with the horses, sir?"

As Malcolm stepped from the carriage, Aldith turned to the owner of the vehicle. "Would it not be easier if we cleared the road ourselves—the five of us, working together?"

The woman snorted. "My dear, such labor is for the commoners, not for a lady such as myself. Nay, we will not clear the road. Matthew will hire peasants for the task."

Fifteen minutes later, Matthew approached the carriage. "The horses are safely across, my lady. They are ready when you are."

Lady Katherine sighed heavily. "If we must, we must." Standing slowly to her feet, she stepped down from the carriage. Aldith and Gavin followed.

Fifty yards from the coach, the road was blocked by a mound of boulders. The rockslide was nearly four feet high. Gavin turned and looked behind the coach. Just as Matthew had said, a second rockslide had blocked the road in that direction as well. The coach was boxed in, unable to go anywhere until the boulders were cleared away.

"This way, my lady." Matthew led the little party carefully across the rockslide, though Lady Katherine complained the entire way. When they reached Malcolm and the two horses, she seemed to perk up.

"You and Malcolm will ride that one," she said to Gavin. "Aldith and I will ride this one. I'm afraid that we will have to ride bareback as the commoners do. Matthew, help us up."

Matthew led one horse close to a large boulder and then assisted his lady in climbing on the animal's back. Lady Katherine sat sideways, looking annoyed and very uncomfortable. Aldith sprang up on the rock and scrambled to the back of the horse unassisted. Malcolm leaped astride the second horse and Gavin climbed up behind him.

"We're off, then," Lady Katherine announced. "Matthew, don't dawdle with the task of clearing the way for the coach. Come for us as quickly as possible."

"Aye, my lady." Matthew bowed and hurried back toward the stranded coach.

The four travelers had ridden just two or three furlongs when they came upon another difficulty. The horses had rounded a bend in the road when Malcolm reined to a stop and exclaimed, "Oh, bother! Look at this."

There in front of them was yet another huge rockslide.

Boulders as big as barns completely blocked the road. "You and Malcolm take the horses around," Lady Katherine ordered Gavin, "while Aldith and I walk." She grunted her disgust with the situation. "Matthew can never take the coach through here. He'll have to find another route."

"Raise your hands in the air," a rough voice snarled, "and get down from the horses. We'll just take those fine animals, if you don't mind."

Fear swept over the four travelers as two men with crossbows appeared from the brush at the side of the road. "Get down from the horses," one man repeated, as both bandits pointed their loaded weapons at Gavin and Malcolm.

"Highwaymen!" Lady Katherine moaned. "As if this day wasn't bad enough, now we're being robbed by highwaymen!"

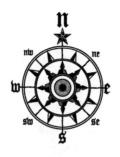

Chapter Nine

"Get down from the horses," the taller highwayman repeated, continuing to point his crossbow at Gavin and Malcolm. "Give us the horses and no one will get hurt."

"You'll never get away with this," Lady Katherine snarled. "The King will have you hunted down and hung for this crime."

The bandit gave her a look of disgust. "Silence, woman, or I'll send the first bolt your way." To the surprise of her companions, the woman fell silent.

"You first," one robber said, gesturing to Gavin. "Get down slow and easy." Gavin complied.

"Now you, sir." Malcolm slid to the ground.

"You're next, lovely," the robber told Aldith. "Slow and easy, now." He extended a hand, but she ignored it and jumped to the ground.

The bandit stepped closer to the horse. "And now you, my lady, without any fuss or bother, right? Just slide down slow and easy like your companions. There now, that's a good woman." He extended a hand to help her down.

Lady Katherine leaned toward the man and then lost her balance, toppling from the horse to land directly on the man, knocking him to the ground. His companion leaped backwards, swinging his crossbow from side to side in a threatening gesture. "Nobody move!" he shouted. "Stay where you are!" And then to Lady Katherine, "Would you get off him, woman? You've nearly squashed the life out of him!"

The woman stood to her feet, angry and embarrassed, but wisely refrained from saying a single word. The robber got up from the ground, moving slowly as if in pain. His lip curled in disgust as he flashed her an angry look, but he said nothing. Both men leaped astride the horses and rode swiftly from the clearing.

"Is everyone all right?" Malcolm asked. The others answered in the affirmative.

"Let's send a petition of thanksgiving," Gavin suggested, "and then we need to make our way across this rockslide."

"So we're back to walking," Aldith grumbled good-naturedly, when they had safely crossed the second rockslide. "The carriage ride didn't last long, did it?"

Lady Katherine's face was a mask of fury. "How can King Emmanuel allow this?" she snarled, though to no one in particular. "Does he expect me to walk the entire way to this wretched mountain? Does he not know who I am?"

"My lady, if I may be so bold as to say so, you should be thankful," Malcolm told her.

"Thankful?" The woman snorted in disgust. "Thankful? We were just robbed, sir! My horses were taken, and now we shall have to walk to Mount Thelema. How can you possibly say that I should be thankful? That's absurd, sir!"

"We can be thankful that none of us were hurt," the cobbler replied quietly. "We can be thankful that the highwaymen took only the horses. We can especially be thankful that they were the ones doing the robbing, and not us. And lastly, we can be thankful that the quest for Mount Thelema was not hindered."

"Not hindered? We are walking, sir." She said the word "walking" as if it were distasteful.

"Aye, but we are walking, my lady," Malcolm replied quietly. "We are still able to continue the quest for the sacred mountain, and for that we can be thankful."

Lady Katherine did not reply, but her face showed that she was disgusted with the cobbler's words.

The four travelers walked for nearly two hours. At last, Lady Katherine sank to a sitting position on a fallen log at the roadside. "I can't go another step," she declared. "We have to rest for awhile." She eyed the western sky, noting that the sun was dropping behind the distant mountain range. "Night is coming fast. Where do you suppose that we will spend the night?"

"We do not know yet, but our King has planned it already," Malcolm replied. "He will provide lodging for us."

Gavin took out his book, removed a parchment, and sent a petition to the Golden City.

> "*His Majesty, King Emmanuel:*
> *As you already know, my Lord, there are now four of us traveling to Mount Thelema that we might know your will for us. Night is coming fast, and as yet we have no lodging. Please guide us to the lodging that you have prepared.*
> *Your son, Gavin.*"

He rolled the parchment tightly, and then released it to watch it shoot over the treetops in a thin streak of silver light. Aldith dropped to a seat beside him. "To think that your petition is already in the throne room of the Golden City," she said quietly. "It's amazing."

Gavin nodded. "Aye, that it is."

Aldith looked past him and a look of utter amazement swept over her features. "Look! What is that?"

All four travelers stared. Two or three furlongs to the south, an enormous stone wall was visible above the trees, and, above the wall, enormous towers and turrets and rooftops. "It's a city," Malcolm said, standing with his mouth half open as he gazed at the distant structures. "It has to be. Come on."

Even Lady Katherine made no protest as together the four travelers hurried south through the forest. Moments later they emerged from the trees to stand in astonishment. "That's— that's incredible!" Gavin stammered in wonder. "This must be the largest city in all Terrestria!"

Standing before them was a massive stone wall more than a hundred feet high that stretched in both directions as far as the eye could see, and, in the center, an arched gateway of glistening white marble. On either side of the gateway crouched colossal lions fashioned from deep red granite. A pavement of blue marble led through the center of the arch. The massive iron gates, sixty or seventy feet tall at the very least, stood wide open as if in welcome. Awed by the spectacle, the four travelers crept to the edge of the gates and peered in. A wide boulevard of polished blue cobblestones led directly away from the gates of the city, and, on either side, magnificent buildings of glistening marble flanked the street. Towers and turrets and pillars glistened in the dying sun like polished gold.

"Such beauty," whispered Lady Katherine. "Such grandeur!"

"It's a city built for giants," Aldith breathed in astonishment. "This gateway must be eighty feet tall!"

"It's at least fifty feet to the head of the lions," Gavin declared.

"At the very least," Malcolm agreed.

"But look at the entrances to the buildings," Gavin replied, whispering without realizing it. "They're huge and they're elaborate, but they're made for ordinary people."

"I—I've never seen anything like it," Lady Katherine whispered in awe, and her companions looked at her, for they had learned already that she was not easily impressed. "Look—look at the size of those buildings."

Malcolm took one cautious step through the massive arch. "Where are the city's inhabitants?" he asked in a hushed voice. "There's not a soul around."

"It's so quiet," Aldith observed.

"The Silent City," Gavin replied. "It's incredible, the most magnificent thing I've ever seen. But where are all the people?"

"Dare we—dare we go in?" Lady Katherine was strangely subdued.

Gavin opened his book and turned it in the direction of the Silent City. The pages blazed with light. "Look at my book," he said softly. "I think that King Emmanuel intends for us to enter the city."

"If that be true, then surely we can come to no harm," Malcolm said easily, raising his voice and striding forward.

Gavin stared at him. *Such a change from the timid soul of a few days ago,* he thought.

Together, the four travelers passed through the glistening marble gate and entered the unusual city. Their footsteps on the polished blue cobblestones echoed between the gleaming buildings. On every side, massive walls and towers and pillars and arches soared skyward. Colossal statues and fountains towered over them.

Gavin stopped and looked around suddenly. His companions noticed and stopped also. "What's the matter?" Malcolm asked, dropping his voice.

"Nothing," Gavin replied, "but don't you feel it? There is a strange atmosphere in this city."

"The buildings and statuary are taller than anything we've ever seen," Lady Katherine pointed out, "and the architecture is overwhelming. Structures this massive tend to make any human feel as small as an ant."

Gavin shook his head. "It's more than that," he replied. "There's an eerie atmosphere here, something that—something that I can't quite explain. I feel like an intruder, and I feel like we're being watched, and yet I feel as though someone or something is welcoming us. Do you sense that?"

"I do," Aldith told him. "I feel as if we were intended to visit this city. And I also feel a tremendous sense of peace and joy."

Gavin looked at her. "Exactly! Did King Emmanuel plan for us to come here, or are we being invited into a trap of some sort?"

"Your book indicated that this was the way," Malcolm pointed out.

Gavin nodded. "Then let's explore the Silent City, shall we? Perhaps this is where His Majesty intends for us to spend the night."

Eyes wide with amazement and awe, the four travelers walked slowly down the wide boulevard, silently drinking in the wonders about them. Each felt an overwhelming sense of wonder, almost of dread, and yet, each felt a deep and settled peace. As Gavin had said, it was almost as if some beneficent being was welcoming them to the incredible city.

"Look at the statues," Aldith said, gazing in wonder at a colossal eagle that towered over the street with wings spread at least a hundred feet. "They're beautiful. They're perfect in every detail!"

"Have you noticed that King Emmanuel's coat of arms is

embossed on the face of every building?" Lady Katherine commented. "In addition to the engraving of knights and horses and swords and crowns, the emblem of the cross and crown is engraved above every doorway."

"Look at the hinges and fittings on each door," Aldith told them, pointing at the ornate entrance to the nearest building. "Unless I'm mistaken, they're made of solid gold!"

Gavin stepped close to the doorway and then beckoned the others over. "Have you noticed that the city looks as if it was built just yesterday?"

Malcolm frowned. "What do you mean?"

"There is no sign that humans have ever been here," Gavin explained. "Nothing is worn or damaged in any way! The cobblestones beneath our feet look as if they were polished just before we arrived. There are no scuff marks of any kind. And look at the handles on these doors—no wear marks at all. It's as if the Silent City was built but never occupied."

"Who built it?" Aldith wondered aloud.

"Well," Gavin replied, "apparently it was built to honor Emmanuel. His coat of arms appears on every building."

"The city square is just ahead," Malcolm remarked, pointing. "Let's see what we find there, shall we?"

The four travelers hurried into a vast open plaza at the end of the boulevard and then paused in sheer wonder. Hovering above the square was an enormous golden crown at least forty feet in diameter. The massive diadem was adorned with emeralds and sapphires and diamonds as big as dinner plates. The sunlight reflecting from the lustrous crown splashed across the square with a radiance that reflected from the faces of the buildings around the square. The sparkling gems seemed to flash colored fire. The massive crown was a wonder to behold.

"What holds it up?" Lady Katherine whispered.

"Nothing that I can see," Malcolm replied, gazing up at the colossal crown. "It appears to be simply floating in the air."

"A crown that large would weight tons and tons," Gavin told him. "How could it float in the air?"

The cobbler shrugged. "I have no explanation whatever, lad. I am as mystified as you." The four stood gazing at the incredible sight for several long moments.

"We were going to take a rest, remember?" Lady Katherine said, dropping wearily to a seat on a marble bench at the base of a seventy-foot sculpture of a woman with a parchment in her hands. "Let's take a brief rest and then see about lodging for the night."

Aldith sat down beside her. "I, too, could use a rest."

"The boulevard continues around that bend," Gavin said, pointing across the square. "While you rest, I'd like to see where it leads."

"I'm with you, lad," Malcolm told him eagerly. He turned to the ladies. "We'll be back in a moment or two. Please stay together, and stay in sight of the crown. We don't want to get separated."

Gavin glanced up at the enormous crown. "Look—is the crown rotating?"

"Rotating?" Lady Katherine frowned. "Why would it rotate?"

"I don't know that it is," Gavin replied, "but that large sapphire was directly above the fountain a few moments ago. Now it is slightly to one side. I think the crown is rotating."

"We won't be gone long," Malcolm promised the ladies, changing the subject. "Come on, lad." Together the two men hurried down the wide boulevard and around the bend.

The boulevard led past what appeared to be an apple orchard, and Gavin stepped over to examine the fruit. "These aren't apples!" he called in astonishment to Malcolm. "They're cherries. Cherries as big as apples!"

His companion was examining another section of the orchard. "The apples are over here," he called back. "They're nearly as big as pumpkins!"

Gavin found a field of standing corn and was astounded to find that the ears were as long as his hand and forearm together. He picked one ear and brought it out to show to Malcolm. "Look at the size of this ear," he said excitedly. "And each stalk has at least twenty ears, rather than three or four or five like they normally do." He peeled back the husk and then pinched the bright yellow kernels. "They're soft and ready to eat," he told the cobbler, "not hard and dry like most corn."

"This place is incredible," Malcolm said, gazing about in wonder. "This is the most incredible city I have ever seen." He glanced suddenly at the sky. "Say, it's getting dark quickly. We had better get back to the ladies. I'll pick an apple to show them and then we had better head back."

With Malcolm carrying a huge apple and Gavin carrying the ear of corn, the two hurried back down the boulevard toward the city square where Aldith and Lady Katherine waited. As they turned the corner, the colossal crown came into view, lustrous and striking.

Gavin stopped short at the sight of the empty bench at the base of the seventy-foot woman. "Where are Aldith and Lady Katherine?"

Together Malcolm and Gavin scanned the square for the sight of the two women, but they were nowhere to be seen. Alarmed, Gavin cupped his hands to his mouth and shouted, "Aldith, we're back! Lady Katherine, where are you?"

But there was no answer. Lady Katherine and Aldith had vanished.

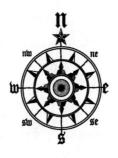

Chapter Ten

Lady Katherine and Aldith had waited patiently on the marble bench at the base of the statue, thankful for the opportunity to sit down and rest their weary feet. "Don't men ever take a moment to sit and rest?" Aldith commented to her companion. "Do they always have to be up and about, poking here and exploring there? After a long day of traveling, you'd think they would be thankful for the chance to sit and rest."

Lady Katherine laughed. "Well, dear, I suppose it depends on the man," she replied. "It seems to me that some do entirely too much resting."

Aldith laughed. She gazed up at the crown, which was almost directly overhead. "You know, I think that Gavin is right—the crown is rotating. I'm sure that it has moved since we've been sitting here."

At that moment, several pairs of large, ornate doors on the magnificent building directly across the square were suddenly thrust open. Beautiful music poured forth from the open doorways, enchanting and inviting. Aldith looked at Lady Katherine. "What in Terrestria?"

"I have no idea," the woman replied in a strange voice. "One never knows what to expect in this city."

Aldith rose to her feet. "I'm going to take a quick look."

"Do you think that's wise, dear?"

"Come with me," Aldith invited, seizing Lady Katherine's hand and pulling her to her feet. "We shall just take a quick look."

Together the two women crept across the empty square, drawn irresistibly by the enchanting music. The fear of the unknown tugged at Aldith's consciousness, but she pushed the apprehensions to the back of her mind. Timidly they mounted the steps of the wide portico and approached the nearest entrance.

Aldith's hand flew to her mouth. "Oh, my!"

The scene before them was breath-taking. They were standing at the entrance to an elaborate banquet hall so vast that they could not see the far end. The walls were of ivory and inlaid with golden etchings. Immense crystal chandeliers hung high overhead, gleaming with twinkling lights like a myriad of distant stars. Row after row of linen-shrouded banquet tables lay before them, complete with ornate place settings. A quick glance showed that tens of thousands of dinner guests were expected. The entire glittering scene was reflected in the mirror surface of the polished marble floor.

Aldith's heart pounded with anticipation. "Have you ever seen anything like it?" she asked quietly.

Lady Katherine slipped into the vast banquet hall and approached a table. "The tableware is not of silver," she whispered, seemingly in shock. "Every utensil is of gold, solid gold! The finest china, the finest crystal…" her voice trailed off as if she were too overwhelmed to continue.

Aldith was at her side in a moment. "Look at the sumptuous meal," she whispered. "Roast pheasant and duck, and so hot it's steaming. Veal and mutton and vegetables of all varieties, and fresh breads. Jellies and sauces and fritters…it's a feast fit for a king! And so many, many place settings! It's as if all of Terrestria is to be invited!"

Bewildered, she looked at Lady Katherine. "What does it all mean, my lady?"

"I'm sure that I don't know," the woman replied. "Perhaps we should hurry back and find the men. This might be a place of danger."

"Oh, I'm sure that it's not," Aldith said softly, gazing about in wonder at the vastness of the magnificent banquet hall. "There's a feeling of peace here, and contentment, and…and joy! I could stay here for a thousand years!"

"We really must be going," her companion insisted, seizing her hand and pulling her toward the entrance. "We still do not know anything at all about this extraordinary city. Let's go back to the city square and wait for the men."

Aldith and Lady Katherine emerged from the banquet hall to find Gavin and Malcolm dashing toward them. "Aldith," Gavin called, overcome with relief. "Are you all right?"

They met on the portico of the banquet hall. "Wait until you see what we have found," Aldith gushed. "You won't believe your eyes!"

"It's the most amazing part of this city yet," Lady Katherine agreed.

Together they led the two men to the doors of the banquet hall and then stood to one side. Without hesitation, Gavin and Malcolm stepped into the vast chamber and then stopped, open-mouthed. Aldith laughed at their reaction.

"What does this mean?" Gavin asked. "There must be thousands of places here, and a hot meal at every single one!"

"Tens of thousands," Malcolm corrected.

"But there's no one here," the youth continued. "Thousands

and thousands of sumptuous meals, yet there is no one here to eat them! What does it all mean?"

Malcolm strode between the ornate tables, and Gavin and the others followed. "Look," Malcolm said, pointing to a place where a golden knife and fork rested on an empty plate, "there's a meal that has been eaten."

"And there's another," Gavin replied, pointing to yet another empty plate.

"Here's one that's half-finished," Aldith chimed in. "And there's another that has been eaten completely."

Gavin paused and scanned the rows of table. "I see others that have been finished or are half-finished," he announced, "but most have not even been touched. The food is hot and looks delicious. But who prepared it—and for whom?"

"This is the most fascinating thing that I have ever seen," Lady Katherine declared, "but perhaps we should leave before someone comes."

Gavin reached out and picked up a piece of dark bread. "It's still hot from the oven," he told the others. Cautiously, he sniffed the bread. "Smells delicious, too."

"Let's leave before someone comes," Lady Katherine said again in a plaintive voice. "We are intruders here, and the master of this city may not take kindly to our intrusion. I say again—this may be a place of danger."

"It's too late," Aldith told her. "Someone is coming, and I fear that we have been discovered." At the far end of the vast banquet hall, a tall figure arrayed in white was hurrying toward them.

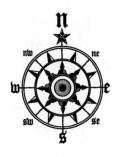

Chapter Eleven

The four travelers stood rooted to the spot as the figure in white hurried across the vast banquet hall toward them. As the person drew closer they could see that it was a woman dressed in a long, flowing white gown that trailed behind her as if blown by a gentle breeze. Long, blonde hair framed a lovely face that now wore a friendly, cheerful smile of greeting.

"Welcome," the woman cried. "Welcome to the City-That-Was-Never-Built. We are delighted that you are finally here."

"Where are we?" Malcolm asked boldly. "My lady, what is this place?"

"You are in the City-That-Was-Never-Built," the woman repeated. "Tonight you are to be the guests of His Majesty. He has prepared lodgings and provisions for your every comfort. Welcome! I trust that your journey was a pleasant one?"

"The City-That-Was-Never-Built," Gavin repeated. "We don't understand, my lady. If the city was never built, why are we here now?"

"I'll explain in a moment," the white lady assured him with a gentle smile. "Gavin, you and Malcolm will lodge together tonight, as will Aldith and Katherine."

"Lady Katherine," the countess corrected her. "I am the

Countess of Windsoar."

The white lady smiled at her as one might smile at a young child. "My dear," she said gently, "there are no titles of nobility in the family of King Emmanuel. As a daughter of the King, you are a princess. Is that not enough? And, of course, you are accompanied on your quest by two princes and another princess."

Lady Katherine stiffened at this rebuke and her face reddened with anger, but then, after a moment, she bowed her head contritely. "Forgive me," she whispered.

"My lady, how do you know our names?" Gavin asked.

The lady smiled again. "It is my business to know these things. I am sent to assist you in your quest for Mount Thelema. My name is Delight."

Gavin was stunned. "Then you know all about us."

"Only what His Majesty wants me to know," she replied.

"What—what is this place?" The question came from Aldith. "The banquet has been prepared for thousands, but there is no one here! This is the most magnificent banquet we have ever seen, but why is no one here to enjoy it?"

"This is the Banquet of Joy," Delight explained. "King Emmanuel has provided the Banquet of Joy for each of his children, but they only partake when they yield themselves to his will."

"But there are thousands of settings," Gavin blurted, "and only a few meals have been eaten."

"Tens of thousands," Malcolm corrected.

Delight smiled. "Actually, there are millions. This banquet hall extends for miles and miles."

"But if the Banquet of Joy has been provided for all of Emmanuel's children, why are there so few who have partaken?"

"The Banquet of Joy is an endless provision from the King, and continues throughout all of life. But as I mentioned, only those who are following the King's will may partake."

She smiled sadly, wistfully. "Oh, that Emmanuel's children could see the banquet they are missing when they scramble for the scraps and crumbs of their own happiness, rather than yielding to the will of their King and enjoying his bounty!"

"You called this the City-That-Was-Never-Built," Gavin told her, "yet you did not tell us how the city got its name. Would you tell us now?"

"The City-That-Was-Never-Built is a replica of the Golden City," Delight began.

"The Golden City of the Redeemed?" Gavin interrupted.

The white lady nodded. "The home of King Emmanuel. The City-That-Was-Never-Built was patterned after The Golden City of the Redeemed. When His Majesty created Terrestria, he intended for its inhabitants to live in his presence. Terrestria was to be a land of prosperity, peace, and incredible joy. The original inhabitants were people of great strength and beauty, incredible intellect, and amazing abilities. The King planned for them to live in perfect harmony with him and with each other, dwelling in lands of wealth and splendor, of which the City-That-Was-Never-Built is a token."

Delight sighed, and then continued. "But alas, as you know, the original inhabitants of Terrestria listened to the lies of Argamor and rebelled against Emmanuel. In so doing, they lost much of their strength and beauty, their intellect, and their abilities. Terrestrians today are but a shadow of what they would have been had they not rebelled against their King."

"And the City-That-Was-Never-Built is what the cities of Terrestria would have been like."

"Exactly," Delight replied. "When the rebellion took place

and was quashed, a curse was placed upon the kingdom of Terrestria for all of time. Only when the King returns to Terrestria will the curse be removed." She smiled at Malcolm and Gavin. "You saw some of the fruits and vegetables that were produced within the city. What did you think of them?"

"They were incredible!" Gavin exclaimed. "Never before have we seen anything like them. The cherries were as big as apples, and the apples as big as pumpkins!"

"All of Terrestria used to produce in such bounty," she told them. "Once the curse is removed from Terrestria, the ground will again yield richness such as you have seen."

"If the City-That-Was-Never-Built has not been built, then how did we see it?" Aldith questioned. "We are in it now. Are you telling us that this city does not exist, that we are not really here?"

Delight laughed. "This is hard to explain to mortals," she replied. "Let's see—how should I say this? The arch and the gate were built, but nothing else. But King Emmanuel designed the gate so that any and all who approach it see and experience the city as though it were there. One day, when Emmanuel returns to Terrestria to reign for a thousand years, this city will be built as a tribute to the glory and splendor of His Majesty and his Golden City."

"So when we passed through the gate, we stepped into the future?" Malcolm asked.

"Aye, in a way, and yet that is not completely accurate." She sighed. "As sons and daughters of Adam and Eve, you would not be able to comprehend it should I explain the matter fully. Someday you shall again have full intellect and full knowledge, and then you shall understand the matter perfectly."

"It's a bit confusing right now," Katherine admitted.

Delight nodded. "As I knew it would be. Let's move on to other matters, shall we?"

"I have a question," Gavin spoke up. "What is the giant crown that we saw suspended in the sky above the city square?"

"Emmanuel's Crown is actually an elaborate timepiece," Delight replied. "It was designed to remind the city's inhabitants that their time belongs to their King and should be spent for his glory."

"A timepiece? How does it tell time?"

"You may not have noticed it, but the crown actually rotates slowly, one full revolution every hour. The front of the crown has a large sapphire that is engraved with Emmanuel's coat of arms, the cross and crown. At the top of each hour the sapphire points due north, directly to the front gates of the Golden City."

"That would mark the minutes," Gavin reasoned, "but how are the hours designated?"

"One jewel appears at each hour, thus marking the hours. There is no timepiece like this in the Golden City, of course, for time is not measured there."

"This entire city is incredible," Katherine said, slowly shaking her head. "Absolutely incredible."

Delight smiled. "If we had the time and you had the capacity to comprehend, I could show you delights and wonders such as you cannot imagine! Aye, your King gives the best to those who choose to do his will."

"I have one more question," Aldith said. "Your name is Delight—how are you so named?"

"As a servant to His Majesty, my greatest delight is to follow Emmanuel's will and do his bidding," the white lady replied. "Believe me when I say that there is great delight in doing the will of Emmanuel. Hence, I was given the name Delight."

With a sweep of her hand she included all four of her guests.

"Come. You must be hungry and tired after your journey, and your King has made provision for your needs. Follow me, if you please."

The four travelers followed Delight from the magnificent banquet hall, across the vast city square, and up the glistening black marble steps of a building with tall, stately white marble pillars. Passing between the pillars, they crossed a wide portico and passed through an ornate silver door with embellishments of solid gold. They entered an anteroom with elegant, colorful banners gracing the walls. The colors of the banners were reflected in the floor of polished black marble.

Crossing the anteroom, they passed though massive mahogany double doors and entered a small but elegant dining room with a fountain against one wall. A single, linen-draped table stood beneath a crystal chandelier ablaze with light. The table was set for four, with a steaming meal already in place in the center.

"The Master would invite you to come and dine," Delight said simply.

As the four took seats around the table, she told them, "This meal has been prepared especially for you, with the rigors of your journey in mind. Please, partake of the King's bounty. I will return when you are finished."

Gavin sent a petition of thanksgiving to King Emmanuel and then the four hungry travelers helped themselves to a meal of roast venison and pheasant, broiled poultry, fresh garden vegetables, and various breads, pastries, and other baked delights. Fruit jellies and sauces completed the delicious meal. Within minutes, the diners had satisfied their appetites, and yet, there was plenty more.

"Is this city enchanted, or is everything in this place as excellent as what we have experienced today?" Katherine asked.

"I have enjoyed the finest culinary delights that Terrestria has to offer, and yet, nothing that I have ever eaten compares with what we have enjoyed tonight. Did you notice—the flavors were so rich, so delightful, and so satisfying."

"Aye," Malcolm agreed, "this was indeed the finest meal that I have ever eaten."

Delight swept into the room at just that moment. "I trust that you have enjoyed the bounty provided by our King," she said sweetly. "I know that you are tired, and if you will follow me, I shall show you the chambers that His Majesty has provided for your rest."

Ten minutes later, Gavin lay in absolute comfort in the center of the biggest, most luxurious bed he had ever seen. The pillow was the softest and the fattest he had ever touched and he turned his head this way and that, trying to find the best position. Across the room, Malcolm the cobbler was dozing off in a similar bed. "Malcolm?" Gavin whispered.

"Unh?" Malcolm was nearly asleep.

"When I first met you, sir, you seemed to have some real fears and reservations about finding Mount Thelema, but it seems that that has changed for you. Do you have any reservations now?"

"None whatever, lad," the cobbler replied, opening his eyes and perking up a bit. "In the last few days I have seen the goodness of my King. I have seen his provision for our needs and his guidance in our journey. In truth, lad, I have felt his presence and experienced the joy that comes from seeking him. If life is this good on the way to Mount Thelema, just think what it will be like after we find Emmanuel's will for us and start following it! I can't wait!"

Gavin laughed. "I agree. But do you suppose that as we travel to Mount Thelema and seek Emmanuel's will, we are actually doing his will? Perhaps that is why we are experiencing such peace and joy."

"Aye," Malcolm agreed. "I think you are right, lad." With these words, he closed his eyes and soon was fast asleep.

※

"It has been my pleasure to have you visit the City-That-Was-Never-Built," Delight told them the next morning after a hearty breakfast. "May I wish you the King's blessings on your quest for Mount Thelema."

"You have been a most gracious hostess," Katherine assured her. "Thank you for the warm welcome and the generous hospitality."

"It was provided by the grace of your King," the white lady told them. "As you seek his will, his provision will follow you all the way to the sacred mountain."

She looked them over as a mother would before sending her children on a journey. "I have a gift for each of you. Malcolm, Katherine, and Aldith, I have a copy of His Majesty's book for each of you. You have been following Gavin's directions from his book, and that is good, for he has led you aright, but you need to find Mount Thelema by seeking guidance for yourselves from the book."

With these words, she handed each of the three a leather-bound book. "Treasure this book, for it is the King's word to you. It will indeed be a lamp unto your feet and a light unto your path. Follow its guidance carefully and completely, for through this very book is Emmanuel's will revealed."

"Thank you, my lady," Aldith, Katherine, and Malcolm said as they received the gift.

"The book is also your defense against attacks by Argamor

and his forces," the white lady told them. "He does not want you to find Mount Thelema and he will oppose you. Victory is assured when you use the book to defeat this wretched foe."

"Katherine," Delight continued, "I have a haversack of the King's provisions for you. Until yesterday, when your carriage and your horses were taken from you, you have always been proud and self-sufficient. His Majesty allowed your carriage to be taken that you might learn to depend on him, rather than on yourself."

Katherine bowed her head as she received the haversack. "Thank you, my lady."

Delight turned to Gavin. "And finally, Gavin, I have a gift for you. It is by far the smallest, and yet by far the heaviest." She handed him an ornate golden ring set with three brilliant sapphires. "You have been chosen to lead this group on the quest for Mount Thelema. Your heart is yielded to the heart of your King, and you have already proven yourself as a man who follows His Majesty's book. Ordinarily, Malcolm would have been chosen to lead, as he is the eldest male, but the ring of responsibility has been placed upon your hand. Are you capable of handling such a responsibility?"

"Nay, my lady, for I am young and inexperienced," Gavin replied immediately. "I have no ability as a leader. Perhaps the ring should go to Malcolm."

"Excellent!" The white lady seemed delighted with his answer. "Your response shows that you are not proud or self-willed, and that you recognize your own inadequacies and will therefore look to King Emmanuel and his book for guidance. I now understand why His Majesty chose you as the leader."

She turned to Malcolm. "I trust that you, sir, are not affronted by His Majesty's choice of Gavin as your leader."

The cobbler shook his head. "I trust that my heart is yielded to my King as well, my lady, and that his will is my greatest desire. If he has chosen Gavin to lead, my heart rejoices in that decision."

"Well said, sir," Delight replied.

"We thank you, Delight, for your generosity to us," Katherine told the white lady, as she embraced her. "Your help and your gifts have encouraged our spirits and your counsel has changed our hearts. We are grateful."

Delight smiled graciously. "Have a blessed journey. I was delighted to have made your acquaintance."

"She was appropriately named, was she not?" Aldith commented, as the four travelers hurried down the wide boulevard of polished blue cobblestones. "She was a delight to be around."

"She delights to be in the will of her King, and that is what makes her such a delightful person," Gavin replied.

"Oh, look!" Katherine cried out, as the four travelers reached the glistening gate of the City-That-Was-Never-Built, "how did we miss those?"

Just inside the city wall, situated on either side of the archway, were beds of brilliant-hued roses of all colors. Just as with everything else in the city, the flowers were huge and the plants towered over the visitors. Malcolm reached up and carefully grabbed a stem, pulling a crimson rose down toward him. "No thorns!" he exclaimed. "Incredible! And each blossom is the size of a melon!"

"Magnificent," Katherine responded, "just like everything else in this city!"

The four travelers passed through the arched gateway and then paused for one last look at the colossal lions. "What a magnificent city," Gavin said quietly. "I've never seen anything like it."

Walking parallel to the wall of the great city, together they started toward the forested hillside three or four furlongs in the distance. "Are we going the right way?" Aldith asked.

"Allow me," Malcolm said, with a huge smile. Pulling his book from within his cloak, he opened the pages and turned them toward the forest. "This is the way," he assured the others. "On to Mount Thelema!"

"On to Mount Thelema," Gavin, Aldith, and Katherine echoed.

As they reached the edge of the forest, Gavin paused. "We each have our own book," he told the others. "Let's pause in the shade of these woods and read the King's words for a few minutes, just to direct our hearts and spirits to seeking the King's will. If we will spend this time in the book, we shall be the stronger for it on this quest."

"You were chosen as the leader," Katherine said agreeably, "and we will follow your counsel. This would also be a good time for each of us to send petitions to the King seeking his guidance and protection on the quest."

Each found a quiet place under the trees and began to read the King's words. As they read, a beautiful white dove flew from tree to tree, gently whispering words of faith and encouragement. After the quiet interlude, renewed in their purpose and strengthened in their faith, they joyfully rose to their feet to resume their journey. Overwhelmed by a sense of the King's presence, Gavin sang a song of praise to Emmanuel and his rich baritone voice resounded through the forest. His companions joined in.

As they walked from the peaceful solitude of the secluded glen, they found themselves face to face with a score of knights arrayed in dark armor. Each knight's shield bore the emblem of the red dragon, Argamor's coat of arms. "Not another step!"

the leader of the dark nights challenged. "One wrong move, and we shall send our bolts and arrows through your hearts!" As he spoke, several of his men aimed their bows and crossbows at the four terrified travelers.

"What are we to do?" Malcolm moaned. "Now we shall never reach Mount Thelema."

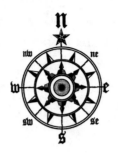

Chapter Twelve

The leader of the dark knights stepped closer, aiming his crossbow directly at Gavin's throat. "Where are you and your company going?" he demanded.

"We are on a quest for Mount Thelema," Gavin answered evenly. "Do not seek to detain us, for we are traveling in the authority and the power of the name of His Majesty, King Emmanuel."

The dark knight spat on the ground. "In the name and the authority of Argamor I order you to turn around and go back from whence you came."

"We will continue on our quest for the sacred mountain," Gavin replied without fear. "You cannot oppose us, for the name of Argamor has no authority over us. We are the children of Emmanuel."

The dark's knight's face contorted with anger. "Then you shall die upon this very spot," he raged, "for no one defies me and lives to tell about it!" With an angry snarl he raised his crossbow and fired a shot at Gavin's heart.

The speeding bolt struck Gavin's Shield of Faith, which harmlessly deflected the missile. Gavin's book was in his hand, so he swiftly slashed through the air with it, transforming it into a powerful sword. With one quick thrust of the sword he ended the dark knight's life and then stepped back to join his companions. "Draw your swords," he said urgently. "The enemy is upon us!"

"There are a score of them," Malcolm quavered, reverting to his old ways of fear and doubt. "There are only four of us—we don't have a chance!"

"A score minus one," Gavin corrected, "and we are armed with His Majesty's own invincible sword, before which the enemy cannot stand. Draw your swords, all of you!"

"Prepare to die, knave," one dark knight snarled. "You have slain our leader, and for this you will pay with your blood." The dark knights surrounded the four travelers, grinning evilly with anticipation.

"What are we going to do?" Aldith cried.

"Draw your sword and prepare to slay some dark knights," Gavin replied fiercely. "Now—draw your swords!"

Slowly, almost reluctantly, his three companions complied.

"Surrender or die!" a dark knight cried. "Drop your swords, or you will not leave this wood alive!"

"Fight only in the power of Emmanuel's name," Gavin urged in a low voice. "If we fight in our own strength, we will be vanquished, for they are more in number than we. His name will bring victory."

"Gavin..." Katherine began in a plaintive voice, but Gavin interrupted her.

"Get your sword up! We will not wait for them to attack us—we will attack first! Ready...charge! For the glory of Emmanuel!" Swinging his invincible sword with all his might, the brave youth charged straight into the ranks of the enemy, and they fell back before the furious onslaught. Malcolm, Aldith, and Katherine stood rooted to the spot, watching in open-mouthed astonishment as the dark knights retreated before the power of Gavin's sword.

Finally, Malcolm could take it no longer. "For the glory of Emmanuel!" he cried, leaping into the fray and swinging his sword fiercely. At the first strike, his sword penetrated the armor of his adversary, and the man retreated quickly, mortally wounded. Soon the cobbler was facing four knights at the same time, and his sword flashed like silver lightning as he battled ferociously.

Aldith turned to Katherine. "We bear the same sword of Emmanuel!" she cried. "Come on!"

Shoulder to shoulder, the four travelers-turned-warriors advanced across the clearing, driving the dark forces back before them. Three dark knights now lay dead upon the ground, and others were wounded. "For the glory of Emmanuel!" Gavin cried. "Remember that we battle only in his name and for his glory!"

Several dark knights rushed straight at them at that moment, dividing their group and bowling Aldith over by the sheer force of the unexpected assault. She tripped and fell headlong, dropping her sword. A dark knight raised his sword, intending to end her life. "Gavin!" she screamed in terror.

Gavin raised his sword, and, seeing that he would not reach Aldith's adversary in time, hurled the powerful weapon with all his might. Like an arrow from a longbow, the sword flew straight to its mark, penetrating the enemy's shield and wounding him mortally. Gavin leaped forward with the speed of a panther, striking the man squarely in the shoulder and bearing him to the ground. He retrieved his sword and ended the dark knight's life.

Aldith grasped her own sword and leaped to her feet, but Malcolm and Katherine were already standing over her, swords drawn and ready to defend her at any cost. "Thank you," Aldith gasped.

At that moment, a barrage of bolts and arrows flew through the air toward the tight cluster of Emmanuel's warriors. To the astonishment of everyone who witnessed it, four Shields of Faith sprang into action of their own accord, deflecting each and every missile harmlessly to the ground.

"We are going to charge them," Gavin instructed his companions. "Follow me—ready? Now!" Shouting the name of his King, Gavin leaped directly at the line of dark knights. His sword flashed like lightning, ending the lives of one, two, three, four dark knights in quick succession. His three companions were right beside him, battling with equal ardor.

It was too much for the dark knights. With screams of terror, the few that were left turned and ran for their lives.

Panting with the exertion of the battle, Gavin raised his sword to the heavens in triumph, and then lowered the point of the blade to the ground. "All praise to Emmanuel!" he cried. "His name has gotten us the victory!"

"All praise to Emmanuel!" his companions echoed. The woods rang with their shouts of victory.

Breathing hard, Malcolm approached Gavin and thumped him on the shoulder. "Thank you for standing in the face of adversity, lad," he said. "But for you, I would have run in defeat."

Gavin grinned. "The name of your King won you the victory," he said humbly.

"We should thank him for it," Katherine suggested. All held their swords against their sides until they changed into books and then each removed a parchment and sent a petition of thanksgiving to the Golden City.

"This was a complete victory," Malcolm exulted. "In spite of their superior numbers, they were not able to stand before us."

"Aye, but we must be alert and watchful," Gavin warned.

"Many times, after a victory, we tend to let down our guard and the enemy comes back in force to win back the victory. We must not allow that to happen."

Malcolm nodded to show that he understood.

"Where's Aldith?" Katherine suddenly cried. "Gavin, where is Aldith?"

Gavin spun around and his heart sank as he scanned the clearing. In an instant, he knew the awful truth: somehow, in their flight, the dark knights had taken the beautiful young girl. Knowing the futility of his actions, he nevertheless threw back his head and called, "Aldith! Aldith, where are you?"

But there was no answer; Aldith was gone.

"We've searched the woods thoroughly," Malcolm soberly told Gavin a short while later, "but there is absolutely no sign of the dark knights. No tracks, no broken brush or twigs—nothing. Nary a sign or track for us to follow to determine which way they went. It's as if they have vanished...simply vanished, I tell you."

Gavin cringed, and Malcolm gave him a sympathetic look. Gavin took a deep breath. His hands trembled. "But there must be something," he said hopelessly. "They couldn't have just disappeared."

"I'm sorry, lad. There's nothing."

"But Aldith couldn't have just vanished," Gavin insisted. "She wouldn't have gone with them willingly, so they would have had to carry her... or drag her! She must have left some sign."

Malcolm sighed heavily. "An expert woodsman or hunter might be able to find something, but you and Katherine and I, well..."

"We need His Majesty's help," Katherine suggested. "Gavin, let's send petitions. For Aldith, and for wisdom for us in finding her."

Gavin nodded. "Never were petitions needed more than now."

At that moment, a young lad ran into the clearing. "I have a message for a man named Gavin," he said, catching sight of the distressed trio. He looked uncertainly from one man to the other. "Which one of you is Gavin?"

"I am," Gavin replied. "Who are you, and what is your message?"

"My name is Thaddeus," the boy replied nervously. "A knight in dark armor gave me a silver coin to give you this." Opening his hand, he presented Gavin with a tiny, rolled parchment and then turned and dashed away.

Gavin's heart was in his throat as opened the missive and read silently,

> *"Do not try to follow us, for any attempt at rescue will result in the death of the lady. If you wish for her to live, simply return by the way that you have come. If you fail to heed these instructions, the lady will die. We will take great pleasure in ending her life."*

Gavin cringed as he read the words, for at that moment he realized just how much Aldith meant to him. He had known her only a short while, but already she had captured his heart. Her beautiful smile, her cheerful words, her intense love for her King, all these and more had caused him to open his heart to her. And now, the peril she was facing would tear his heart from him. Suddenly he found himself struggling just to breathe.

Malcolm read his facial expression and read his heart. Gently, he reached out and took the terse message from Gavin's trembling fingers. In a moment's time he read it and then folded it closed with one hand. His strong, callused hand rested on the youth's shoulder. "Your King is able, lad," he said quietly, huskily, for already he had discerned Gavin's feelings for the young lady.

"We don't even know where she is, sir," Gavin moaned, overwhelmed with the impossibility of the situation.

"Aye, but your King knows."

"If we try to follow them, they'll kill her!"

"Is not your King able to protect her from the likes of them?"

"A petition, Gavin," Katherine urged. "Let us all send a petition."

Numb with grief, Gavin nodded. "Aye, you are right. You are both right."

Together, the trio opened their books and withdrew parchments. Each wrote a fervent message to King Emmanuel and then released the petitions, watching as the parchments shot above the trees on their way to the Golden City.

"We're not far from the City-That-Was-Never-Built!" Gavin suddenly remembered. "Perhaps Delight can help us."

"In what way?" Malcolm queried.

Gavin shrugged. "She seemed to know everything about everything. Perhaps she would know where they have taken Aldith."

After a brief hike through the woods, the three travelers emerged from the forest. Gavin was in the lead and he stopped and stared in utter dismay. "Would you look at that! Where is the city?"

There on the plain before them stood an enormous arch, glistening and white. The massive iron gates stood wide open as if in welcome. But beyond the gates, there was nothing—no boulevard of blue cobblestones, no gleaming marble buildings, no fountains, no statues, nothing but a vast, empty plain.

Trembling with disappointment, Gavin ran forward and passed through the gates. Sadly, he turned to face Malcolm and Katherine. "But where is the City-That-Was-Never-Built?" he cried in anguish. "It was right here! Right here—less than an hour ago!"

Katherine walked forward to meet him. "The city was never built," she said softly. "Remember?"

Gavin was desperate. "I thought that Delight could help us! But she's not here! How will we find Aldith?"

"Our hope is in Emmanuel, lad, not in the City-That-Was-Never-Built, or in the white lady. Trust him, lad, for he cares and he is able." Malcolm put an arm around Gavin's shoulders and led him back through the colossal gates. "Let's go back to the solitude of the woods. Perhaps it is there that His Majesty will answer our petitions."

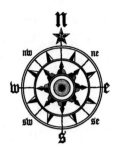

Chapter Thirteen

Gavin's heart cried out as he stared into the campfire, watching the flames leap about like dancers in colorful, shimmering costumes. He sighed. From all evidence, the dark knights had Aldith. How would he and Malcolm and Katherine get her back? They had searched the woods for hours, but had found no clue as to which direction the dark knights had taken her. How could he rescue her if he didn't even know where she was?

He and his companions had sent numerous, desperate petitions to the Golden City, but as yet, there had been no answer from Emmanuel. Could it be that His Majesty did not care that Aldith had been taken—was he too busy with other matters? Why would he not answer?

Gavin shook his head as if to clear such unworthy thoughts from his mind. Emmanuel did care—of that Gavin was sure. But it was so very, very difficult to wait. He swung his sword fiercely, feeling the strength of the steel in his hand, enjoying the flash of reflected firelight as the glimmering blade slashed through the darkness of the night. His sword would make mincemeat of the enemy, if only he knew where they were!

"His Majesty will answer, lad." Malcolm's voice was low and gentle, but it startled the youth just the same. "Emmanuel cares for her as much as we do, and he will answer. He will show us where Aldith is and what we must do to rescue her."

Gavin swallowed hard and nodded. "I know, sir, I know. I believe that he will answer. But why does he make us wait—why not answer now? Malcolm, I don't even know where they took her!"

The cobbler smiled sadly. "I know, lad, I know."

With a flash of white plumage, the dove flew down and alighted on a low branch. Gavin rushed to him. "Where is Aldith?" he asked eagerly. "Do you know where she is? Can you take me to her?"

"Aldith is in the hands of the enemy knights, just as you feared," the dove replied. "She is presently being held at their camp just six or eight furlongs due north of here."

"Take me to her!" Gavin begged.

"Not yet," the dove responded. "There is a need to wait. When the moon rises above the treetops, take Malcolm and Katherine with you and follow the footpath that starts at that large rock formation. You shall be able to rescue Aldith with very little effort." Spreading snowy wings, the dove flew away into the darkness of the night.

Gavin turned to Malcolm. "Did you hear that?"

"Aye," Malcolm replied. "Did I not tell you that His Majesty would answer? Now you know where Aldith is, and what to do about it."

Gavin spotted the boulder to which the dove had referred. "Malcolm, let's go," he said urgently. "The trail starts there at that rock."

"You heard the dove," Malcolm replied. "We are to wait until the moon rises above the treetops."

Gavin glanced upward. "But the moon is yet low on the horizon," he argued, spotting a silver glow through the trees. "That could take forever."

"Aye, but we are to wait."

Gavin walked over to the rock formation and easily found the trail. *There's no need to wait until the moon rises,* he told himself impatiently. *There's plenty of light to see the trail. And besides, the darker the night is, the harder it will be for them to see us coming.* He glanced back at Malcolm and Katherine, who both sat by the fire, casually conversing as if they were totally unconcerned with Aldith's plight.

Do they not care about Aldith? he thought angrily. *We don't even know what's happening to her, but they act like it doesn't matter that she has been taken! Well, here's one fellow who cares.*

Bending down, he studied the narrow trail in the obscure light. *I'm not going to wait and give the dark knights a chance to hurt Aldith,* he thought fiercely. *There are only seven or eight of them left—I'll go by myself! Malcolm and Katherine don't seem to care about Aldith, anyway.* Without a word he slipped into the darkness of the night.

Following the narrow path was difficult in the darkness, but Gavin managed. Twenty minutes after he left the campfire, he saw a flickering amber glow through the trees ahead. He was approaching another campfire. Walking slowly and noiselessly, he slipped down the hillside. In the center of a small clearing, a small fire leaped and danced. Seated around the fire were nine—aye, nine, for he counted them—dark knights laughing and talking and drinking from tall pewter steins.

His heart leaped, for there, seated against a tree, was Aldith, bound hand and foot. Her eyes were wide and she looked angry, but apparently she was unharmed. He watched her for a moment and his heart ached. She was less than thirty feet away; if only he could dash through the trees, snatch her up, and run away with her to safety!

"Are you sure you won't have some ale with me, my lovely?"

one of the knights called in Aldith's direction, and the dark knights all laughed.

Gavin glanced at Aldith just in time to see her lift her chin and turn her face away. The knights roared with laughter.

Gavin tightened his jaw and drew his sword. *You won't be laughing much longer,* he thought fiercely. *Emmanuel, help me!*

Leaping to his feet, he charged through the trees, screaming at the top of his voice and swinging the sword with all his might. The dark knights were as startled as Aldith. Rolling away from the fire, they leaped to their feet and scattered like mice fleeing from a cat. Gavin laughed. *This was easier than I anticipated.* He turned toward Aldith and caught a glimpse of horror on her features.

"It is I, Aldith," he said with a laugh, but that was as far as he got. Behind him, a dark knight swung a mace with all his might, and the heavy weapon caught Gavin squarely between the shoulder blades, hurling him forward and slamming his head against a tree. A flash of intense white light seemed to explode in front of Gavin's face and then darkness swept over him.

Gavin awoke to find that the enemy's campfire had gone out. His head throbbed painfully and his back felt as if he had received an energetic kick from a mule. His mouth was dry and gritty. He lifted his head. The moon was overhead now, and there was enough silver light for him to see that the little clearing was spinning crazily. He dropped his head, waiting for the dizziness and nausea to pass.

Where was Aldith? He lifted his head abruptly, but he knew what he would find before he even looked. The place that she had occupied beneath the tree was now empty. Aldith was gone.

He tried to stand, but his knees buckled and he barely managed to catch himself before his face hit the dirt. "Your Majesty," he cried aloud, "why did you not answer? Why did you allow them to take Aldith away? I could have rescued her."

Strong hands gripped his arm just then, and he turned, fearfully, knowing that he was in the clutches of the dark knights. But the face above him was friendly, and relief swept over him as he realized that he was in Malcolm's strong grasp. "It's all right, lad," Malcolm's voice sounded in his ear, and then he felt the strong hands lifting him. Darkness swept over him.

He awoke again to find that he was back at his own campfire. "How—how did I get here?" he asked.

"You didn't walk, lad," Malcolm replied with a wry grin. "I had to carry you every step of the way. Fortunately, there was a bit of moonlight so that I could at least see the trail."

"What—what happened?"

Malcolm was blunt. "You disobeyed the voice of the dove and nearly got yourself killed by the dark knights."

"Where is Aldith?"

"They still have her, lad. You didn't accomplish a thing by going off on your own before the moon was up."

"But it was light enough to see the trail," Gavin protested. "There was no need to wait for the moon."

"The light on the trail had nothing to do with it," another voice answered, and Gavin looked up to see the dove on a branch just over his head. "The dark knights were drinking grog and ale. If you had waited until the moon was above the treetops, they would have all been in a stupor and you and Malcolm could have easily freed Aldith. As it is, you have warned the dark knights of your intentions and they have taken her to the security of one of Argamor's castles. Your task will now be tenfold as difficult as it would have been if you had waited."

Gavin dropped his head. "I am sorry. Forgive me—I beseech you. Perhaps I should now give the ring of leadership to Malcolm."

"There is forgiveness with Emmanuel," the dove replied, "and the ring is still yours, though you now feel unworthy. It would do no good to pass the ring to Malcolm—he will have his share of failures also."

A soft hand touched his face and he looked up into Katherine's worried eyes. "Gavin, are you all right?"

"I'm alive, if that matters," he replied. He looked at Malcolm, and then at the dove. "Where is Aldith now? And what are we to do to get her back?"

"Take your rest until I wake you," the dove replied. "Aldith will come to no harm. When I know that you are ready, I will lead you to the castle where she is now a prisoner."

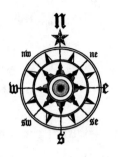

Chapter Fourteen

The night was still dark when Gavin felt a gentle hand on his shoulder. He awoke and sat up instantly, but Malcolm was still stretched out by the fire and Katherine was asleep in the crude lean-to that Malcolm had built for her. He rubbed his eyes. Who had touched him?

"Wake Malcolm and Katherine and follow me," the voice of the dove said, and Gavin looked up to see the celestial bird waiting patiently in a pine tree. "Be sure to take your haversacks."

The youth stood stiffly to his feet. "I think I have a kink in my back from sleeping on the hard ground."

"His Majesty planned better accommodations than these," the dove replied gently. "Had you obeyed my voice, you and your companions would have been afforded the opportunity to enjoy them, and the young lady would now be in your company."

Gavin hung his head.

"Wake your companions."

Gavin did, and the cobbler and the countess sat up, rubbing their eyes and staring at the darkness around them. "Lad, what in Terrestria? It's the middle of the night!"

"The dove wants us to follow him," Gavin said quietly. "We

are to rescue Aldith."

Malcolm took a deep breath and then stood up immediately. "I'm ready."

Katherine stepped forward from the lean-to. "As am I."

"Take your haversacks," the dove prompted, and the three obeyed.

"Follow me."

Twenty minutes later, the dove alighted in an oak on the crest of a steep hill. "Just below us is the Castle of Impurity, a stronghold of Argamor's," the dove informed Gavin, Katherine, and Malcolm, as they caught up. "Aldith is being held in the northwest tower on the inner curtain wall. You are to scale the tower and bring her to safety."

"Climb the tower? But that's impossible!"

"Difficult, but not impossible. His Majesty has already provided you with the means to do so. Look within your pack."

The three unshouldered their packs and looked inside. Malcolm and Katherine found a disassembled crossbow and three sharp bolts in each of their packs, while Gavin found something else—a seventy-foot coil of stout rope with a grappling hook at one end. Warily, he eyed the equipment. "What—what am I to do with this?"

"You are to use the rope to scale the castle walls," the dove answered simply. "Malcolm and Katherine will assemble the crossbows while you are gone."

Gavin's mind was racing. "Scale the walls?" he echoed. "I am to scale the outer wall, lower myself into the barbican, scale the inner wall and the tower, and then return with Aldith the same way? But—but that's impossible!"

"Difficult," the dove replied, "but not impossible. Last night would have been far simpler, would it not, if you had merely waited as you were instructed?"

BOOK ONE: TALES FROM TERRESTRIA

Gavin smiled sheepishly. "Aye." He glanced at Malcolm and then back to the dove. "But I am learning to listen to your voice."

"What are Katherine and I to do?" Malcolm questioned.

"Assemble the crossbows," the dove replied. "Gavin and Aldith will face extreme danger as they leave the castle, and you are to cover their escape."

Malcolm's hands trembled as he began to assemble the weapon.

Gavin crouched in the shadows below the castle wall, thankful that the Castle of Impurity did not have a moat. As the sentry passed by on the wall, the youth ducked lower. "Three minutes, twenty seconds," he whispered. "From the time the sentry turns the far corner, I have three minutes, twenty seconds." He had timed the sentry's pass three times now, and the dark knight's routine had not varied by as much as three seconds. But three minutes, twenty seconds would not be much time to accomplish what he had to do.

He would have to hurl the grappling hook to the top of the wall—hoping desperately that it would catch the first time—climb the rope twenty-six feet to the top of the wall, and then pull the rope up. He would cross the sentry walk, secure the rope around one of the merlons and descend the line, and then free the rope before the sentry passed on another round. He sighed. *That's an awful lot to do in three minutes twenty, even if all goes right. And if something should go wrong, well...*

He waited until the sentry had made one more pass and turned the corner at the far end of the castle. Leaping to his feet, Gavin bolted for the wall, swinging the grappling hook in a wide circle as he ran. As he neared the outer curtain wall he hurled the grappling hook with all his might. The hook sailed upward through the darkness and then broke into the moonlight as it cleared the castle wall. Gavin held his breath. The hook caught—good!

The trembling youth tested the rope by giving it a sharp tug. His heart seemed to stop as the rope came snaking down at his feet and the grappling hook struck the ground nearby. The hook had not caught, after all—that was bad.

Leaning down, he swept his hand back and forth across the darkened ground as he searched for the hook. At last, after an eternity of searching, he found it. Coiling the rope frantically, he swung the hook in circles as he prepared for a second cast. He caught himself just before he released the hook. Too much time had passed—the sentry would soon be coming by. Better to wait until he had passed and then start the cycle over again.

Ninety seconds later, he rose to his feet, swinging the hook, and ran forward. Release! The hook sailed in a perfect arc over the top of the wall. Gavin pulled on the rope. It held fast. He jerked on the rope with all his might. The hook still held fast. He took a deep breath. It was now or never. Hand over hand, he pulled himself up the rope, thankful for the knots every twelve inches or so. Reaching the top of the wall, he pulled himself up until he got an elbow over the merlon to his right. He swung a leg up... and in a matter of seconds he was scrambling across the sentry walk to free the grappling hook.

He crossed the sentry walk, threw the grappling hook down into the darkness of the barbican below the wall, and then dropped the loose end of the rope on the opposite side of the merlon. Once he reached the bottom, the rope would release easily. His heart was in his throat as he leaned over the edge, gripped the rope with both hands, and slid down into the barbican. He was actually inside the castle!

As soon as his feet touched solid ground, he released one end of the rope. Jerking on the end with the grappling hook, he brought the entire rope snaking down into the darkness with him. The free end struck him in the face as it fell, but he hardly felt it. The first step in the dangerous game was accomplished. Crouching in the darkness, he tried to still his racing heart as he waited for the sentry to pass.

The inner curtain wall would be harder—thirty-eight feet—as opposed to the twenty-six feet he had just climbed. The danger would be compounded by the fact that once he started up the wall, he could be spotted by the sentries on either the outer or the inner curtain walls. He opened his book and took out a parchment. Lacking the light to see and the instrument to write a message, he simply rolled the parchment and sent it as a wordless petition. Emmanuel would understand.

When the sentry passed, Gavin counted to twenty and then dashed for the inner curtain wall. The grappling hook caught on the first try—good. Just to be sure, he gave the rope two good hard jerks, but the line refused to budge. Good. Taking a deep breath, he climbed as fast as he could, thankful that the moon had hidden behind a cloud.

Just as he reached the top of the wall and threw a leg over the merlon, the moon came dashing from behind the clouds and bathed the castle walls in brilliant silver light. Gavin's breath caught in his throat. Silhouetted atop the wall as he was, he could be seen by almost anyone inside the castle! Heart racing, he ducked into the shadow of the battlements and waited for several terrifying seconds.

His mind cleared. He should coil the rope while he waited. He freed the grappling hook and looped the rope into loose, open coils. When no one came after many anxious moments of waiting, he crept forward and tried the tower door. It refused to move and he realized that it was barred from the inside.

And now would come the worst part. With the door barred, there was no entrance to the tower from the sentry walk. Either he would have to enter from the bailey, which was unthinkable since it would necessitate a descent down the line and greatly increase his chances of running into the enemy once he entered the bailey, or he would have to scale the tower and enter through the roof. As dangerous as it was, his chances were better if he went through the roof. Standing to his feet on the sentry walk, he hurled the grappling hook up, up, up and over the top of the tower. It caught.

He had decided on an extremely risky maneuver. If he could somehow reach and climb the outer side of the tower, his assault on the tower would be far less noticeable from the sentry walk and from down inside the courtyard of the bailey. Leaning far out into the darkness and gripping the rope as high as possible, he hurled his weight into the rope and swung as far out as possible. Like a spider on a strand of web, he swung around the far side of the tower and then gravity hurled him back toward the structure. As he lifted his feet to brace for the impact, one boot found its way squarely into an arrow loop, the narrow window through which archers could shoot. Incredible!

The rope snapped back, nearly jerking him from the wall, but he stiffened his back and pulled against it just in time to regain his balance and maintain his precarious perch on the tower wall. *Thank you, Emmanuel!*

Clinging desperately to the rope, he paused for a moment to catch his breath. If he could shift the rope above him, he could climb the backside of the tower as he had hoped. But it would be extremely risky. If the grappling hook should break free, well...

He decided to risk it. Leaning forward so that almost all of his weight was on his foot in the arrow loop, he raised his hands and flipped the rope sharply to the right. As his weight shifted back to the rope, his heart pounded with fear. Would the rope hold, or would he fall?

It held.

And then, at that moment, the thought struck him like an arrow from a longbow. *Is this not the second time that I have risked my life on a rope to rescue Aldith? Here I am, terrified of heights, clinging to the tower of an enemy castle!*

Hand over hand, he climbed to the top of the tower. He breathed a sigh of relief as he scrambled over the battlements. He was in the tower, safe—for the moment. Panting with exertion, he knelt in the shadows of the battlements as he caught his breath and rested for a moment. As his heart rate dropped, he freed the grappling hook and then retrieved the rope, arranging it carefully in a neat coil. He crawled carefully across the tower, feeling the roof. At last, his probing fingers found an iron ring. The trap door!

Pausing for a long moment to make certain that his intrusion had not been observed, he pulled with both hands. The trap door opened with the squeak of rusty hinges. He heard a low cry of terror. "Who's there?"

He leaned his face close to the opening. "Aldith—is that you?"

"Gavin?"

"It is I," he called softly, and his heart leaped. Aldith was alive! He had found her!

"Gavin?" Aldith's voice held a tone of hope mingled with disbelief. "Gavin, is that really you?"

"It really is," he replied, and his heart was now singing.

"Where are you? I can hear you, but I can't see you."

"I'm on the roof. Is there anyone in the room with you?"

"Nay, just me."

"Aren't you being guarded?"

"I think there's a knight somewhere below me," she replied, "maybe just inside the door to the sentry walk."

He reached down and in the darkness found the spiraling stairs. His heart pounded with anticipation as he followed the stairs down into the darkness of the solar. As he reached the floor, a shadowy form moved and then Aldith was upon him, squeezing the life out of him in a tearful embrace. "Oh, Gavin! Gavin!"

His heart raced. "There's not a moment to lose," he told her, twisting free from her embrace. "If my entrance was observed, a score of enemy knights could be here at any moment."

He drew his book and transformed it into the sword. "Are you ready? Let's go."

It was then that he heard the dull clank of a heavy chain. "I can't," Aldith sobbed. "I'm chained to the bed."

"Use the Key of Faith," spoke a quiet voice from the darkness, and Gavin looked up in astonishment to realize that the dove was present in the solar. "Use the Key of Faith; it's in your book."

Gavin held his sword against his side until it changed back into the book and then opened the cover to find a lustrous golden key shimmering in the darkness. Eagerly he snatched it from the book and then leaned down toward Aldith's shackles. The moment the golden key touched the iron, the shackles fell to the floor with a loud clank.

"Where's the door?" Gavin whispered, as he replaced the Key of Faith within his book. Closing the book, he transformed it once again into the sword.

The door opened at that moment, and a rough voice called,

"Who's there? Who's there, I say?" A dark knight strode into the chamber with a sword in one hand and a torch in the other. When he saw Gavin he gave a snarl of rage and leaped forward, swinging the sword with all his might.

Gavin raised his Shield of Faith just in time to fend off the blow and then returned the blow with his own sword. The powerful blade caught the dark knight squarely across the chest, knocking him backwards and denting his breastplate, but inflicting no real injury. The guard recovered his balance and then leaped at Gavin, slashing furiously with his sword again and again. Caught off guard by the ferocity of the assault, Gavin was hard-pressed to fend off the unrelenting blows of the sword. In a moment the dark knight had him backed against the wall with nowhere to go.

"Gavin!" Aldith cried, and the dark knight threw a quick glance in her direction.

The split-second diversion gave Gavin the opportunity he needed. Using his sword to thrust aside his opponent's, he lunged at the man, striking him body-to-body with a loud crash of armor. The impact knocked the enemy off balance and he staggered backwards. Gavin followed through with his sword, swinging the invincible weapon in a back-handed move that sent the dark knight to the floor and ended his life.

Gavin seized the guard's torch and dashed to the door. "Come on, Aldith!"

Running down one flight of stairs, they came to a barred door. Gavin threw the torch to the floor and unbarred the door. Silver moonlight flooded the chamber as he opened the door. He and Aldith found themselves on the sentry walk of the inner curtain wall. "The rope! I forgot the rope!"

She stared at him. "What rope?"

"It's up in the tower," he told her. "Quickly—back inside, so you're out of sight. I'll be back in seconds."

Ninety seconds later, Gavin watched as Aldith slid down the rope into the darkness of the barbican. When the rope went slack he knew that she had reached the bottom, and he quickly followed. He freed the rope and coiled it carefully. "How will we get over the outer wall?" Aldith whispered fearfully.

"The same way I came in," he replied, "we'll climb the rope."

"I—I don't think I'm strong enough to do that," she told him.

"Malcolm is waiting outside the outer curtain," he explained. "Together we will pull you up."

"Isn't this the second time you two have done this?" she asked, with a giggle.

He laughed softly, enjoying her presence in spite of the danger they were in. "Aye, fair maiden, but this is the last time. After this, you're on your own!"

"Really, sir," she retorted, pretending to pout.

"Follow me," he whispered. "We still have to get you out of here." Silently, they crossed the darkness of the barbican. As they reached the base of the outer curtain, Gavin crouched in the darkness with Aldith beside him. "Stay still," he whispered. "We have to wait for the sentry to pass."

It was then that he realized the tight spot that they were in. *Three minutes twenty,* he told himself. *There is no way that Aldith and I can both cross the wall in three minutes and twenty seconds before the sentry comes around again! What will we do?* As he waited for the sentry, he quickly sent a wordless petition to Emmanuel.

The sentry approached a moment later, and Aldith gasped as the man passed by on the wall. The sentry paused, leaned over the battlements, and stared hard into the darkness of the barbican. Aldith and Gavin flattened themselves against the wall, hardly daring to breathe. The girl placed her hand on Gavin's arm and he realized that she was trembling uncontrollably. In the silver light of the moon, the sentry was clearly visible, but the barbican was dark and full of shadows, and Gavin hoped desperately that he and Aldith were invisible. But if the guard should call for a torch and come down to investigate…

Satisfied that all was well, the dark knight at last moved on. Aldith gave an audible sigh of relief.

Gavin counted to twenty and then stood to his feet. Raising the grappling iron, he began to swing it in a circle as he prepared to cast it over the wall. Aldith gripped his left arm. "The stairs! Why can't we just use the stairs?"

He stared at her and then turned and looked in the direction that she was pointing. Sure enough, a long flight of stairs led to the sentry walk atop the outer wall. *Why didn't I see those?* "Come on! We've got no time to lose!"

His heart pounded as he and Aldith raced to the top of the wall. He quickly secured the rope and then threw the coils out into the darkness below the wall. "You're first," he told Aldith.

"And just where do you think you're going?" a rough voice snarled. A dark form leaped forward into the moonlight, and Gavin realized too late that the sentry had hidden in the shadows. As the angry knight advanced toward them with sword drawn, Gavin's heart sank. There would be no time to draw his own sword. He and Aldith were trapped.

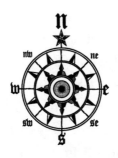

Chapter Fifteen

"Trying to rescue the lady, were you, knave?" the sentry snarled as he advanced toward Gavin with his sword drawn. "Terrible mistake, that was. Now I'll have to run you through before I return the princess to her tower." He laughed. "I thought it was going to be a dull night, I did, but it looks like I will have the pleasure of killing one of Emmanuel's own sons."

Gavin inched his hand toward his doublet, but the dark knight had anticipated the move and was ready for him. "Don't even try it!" he growled, pressing the edge of his blade against Gavin's throat.

"What have you got, Barclan?" a man's voice called, and a second sentry hurried across the sentry walk. His eyes widened when he saw Gavin and Aldith. "Intruders, eh? Good piece of work, Barclan."

"One intruder and one attempted escapee," Barclan corrected his companion. "The young knight here was trying to free the lady."

"Were you, now?" the second sentry taunted. "It didn't go too well, did it?" He stepped close to Gavin, laughing at the look of despair that had appeared in the youth's eyes. "Now don't take it too hard, lad. Barclan here is one of the finest sentries in the castle. You were captured by one of the best." He looked at Barclan, who still held his sword at Gavin's throat. "Want any help taking them back?"

Barclan shook his head. "It's not necessary. I'll simply run this knave through and then escort the lady back to her solar."

"As you wish." The second sentry turned away.

At that moment, a bolt from a crossbow suddenly embedded itself in Barclan's chest, passing cleanly through his chain mail. He fell to the sentry walk with a strangled gasp. The second sentry whirled, drawing his sword as he did, and leaped for Gavin. The terrified youth side-stepped, desperately reaching for his sword but knowing he would never draw it in time.

A second bolt caught the second sentry in the throat just as he lunged for Gavin. His sword fell from his hand to clatter harmlessly on the sentry walk. Seconds later, the crash of armor echoed across the castle as his body struck the stonework of the battlements. Gavin's knees buckled and he sank to the sentry walk, weak with fear as he realized how close he had come to death.

"Hurry, lad!" a familiar voice cried from down below, and Gavin abruptly realized where the unexpected bolts had come from. Gripping the edge of the crenel between two merlons, he pulled himself to his feet.

"You're first, Aldith."

The girl seemed to fling herself into space as she slid down the rope. Gavin was right behind her. "Leave the rope," Malcolm urged, as the pair landed beside him in the darkness. "Let's get out of here!"

"Excellent shooting, sir," Gavin called, as he and Aldith followed Malcolm and Katherine through the darkness. "You saved my life."

"The second shot was Katherine's," Malcolm replied. "Now we both know why His Majesty provided crossbows in our packs. Praise him for it."

"How did the dark knights take you, dear?" Katherine asked Aldith. "Did you not put up a struggle? We could find no tracks anywhere."

"The ground beneath me gave way during the battle with the dark knights," Aldith explained, "and I fell into some sort of a pit or a sinkhole. A dark knight fell with me. He held a dagger to my throat to keep me from calling out until you had left the area."

"But how did he get you out of the woods without us seeing you?"

"The sinkhole led to an underground cavern, and he made me follow that until we came out on the side of the hill quite a distance from where we had fallen in."

"That must have been terrifying."

"I never want to go through it again," the girl replied.

"We're just thankful that you're safely back," Malcolm remarked.

"Are we ever!" Gavin agreed, and then stopped, embarrassed, hoping that his words had not sounded too eager.

The eastern sky was just beginning to glow with the first hints of dawn as the four tired travelers entered their campsite. "Let's get some rest," Gavin told the others. "We'll start out again after we have rested awhile."

"Thank you for rescuing me," Aldith told him quietly. "That was the bravest thing that anyone has ever done! I owe my life to you."

Gavin was thrilled by her words and yet embarrassed at the same time. "Aye, well, praise Emmanuel that it went well," he said, as the blood rushed to his face. "If I had listened to the voice of the dove, things would have been a lot easier!"

BOOK ONE: TALES FROM TERRESTRIA

The four travelers resumed their quest the next morning after a hearty breakfast of trout that Malcolm caught in a nearby stream on a hand line taken from his haversack. The morning was sunny and cool as they started out, and although the day was bright, a swirling mist hovered near the ground. "It's as though we're walking on clouds," Aldith commented.

Gavin's heart was full as they hiked along. *What a journey this has been already! We have seen Emmanuel's provision and protection at every turn, although our own blunders have brought a share of trouble. I wonder how much farther to Mount Thelema? What does His Majesty's will hold for me, and for Malcolm and the ladies?*

He glanced at Aldith, and his heart thrilled as she gave him a radiant smile. *Wouldn't it be grand if the King's will for me included a lady as lovely as Aldith? Wouldn't it be grand if it included Aldith herself!* He shook his head. He would be content with Emmanuel's will, whatever it held, for he had seen glimpses of the King's wisdom and power and now knew that the loving monarch would bestow on him an abundant life, far better than anything he could plan for himself.

"We had better consult the book often today," Malcolm suggested, jolting Gavin from his reverie. "This fog is so thick that we could easily lose our way."

"Unusual, isn't it?" Katherine remarked. "The sun is bright, yet this fog hugs the ground like a blanket. I've never seen anything like it."

The trail began to wind its way up the side of a heather-covered hillside and Gavin consulted his book to check their direction. The fog swirled about their knees and ankles, so thick that they could no longer see the ground. And then, like a wave of the ocean, the fog swept over them and blotted out the sun. Gavin could barely see three feet in front of him.

He stopped to consult the book and Aldith bumped into him. "It's getting awfully thick, isn't it?" she said quietly, and her face betrayed the fact that she was worried. "We can hardly see the trail."

"We have the book," Gavin assured her. "We cannot lose our way as long as we follow it closely."

"Stay close together," Malcolm warned. "It would be easy to get separated in this fog."

A chilling rain began to fall and the travelers wrapped their cloaks about their heads in an attempt to ward off the elements. Soon the trail was wet and muddy. "We'll be chilled by the time we find lodging tonight," Katherine declared.

Moments later Aldith paused on the trail. "Listen!"

Her companions stopped. "What did you hear?"

Aldith frowned. "I don't know," she said slowly. "It sounded like…chains."

"Chains?" Malcolm asked.

"Aye, you know, clanking together like they do."

At that moment they all heard it. From somewhere in the swirling mists ahead came the unmistakable clanking of chains. The four looked at each other in bewilderment. "Now what do you suppose that could be?" Katherine asked of no one in particular.

A tall, black form parted the mists as a powerful horse materialized out of the fog. Seated on his back was a well-dressed merchant. "I beg your pardon, good people," he called cheerfully, as he spotted the four travelers. "Please bear with us as we pass."

Gavin and his companions stepped to one side of the narrow trail to allow the horse to pass. They were completely unprepared for what they saw next. Behind the horse walked a pitiful creature with heavy chains on his arms and legs. Dressed in rags, the figure had dirty, matted hair, and his arms and legs were skeletal. His eyes bore a look of torment and hopelessness as they peered out from an unwashed face covered by a scraggly growth of beard.

Close behind Gavin, Aldith gave a tiny, sobbing moan as she saw the poor wretch. The man turned toward them as he shuffled past, and the travelers' hearts ached as they saw the anguish in the man's face.

Gavin was stunned as a second pitiful soul materialized out of the mists and staggered toward them. Just as pathetic and hopeless as the first figure, this was a woman, and her face portrayed such despair that Gavin could not bear to look upon her. He found himself compelled to drop his gaze until the woman had passed. Aldith began to sob.

And then there were others. Chained together like animals, one by one they filed past the four stunned travelers, shuffling hopelessly, eyes blank and staring, shoulders slumped forlornly as if they had long ago given up all hope. "Slaves!" Aldith spat out the word. "These poor creatures are slaves."

"Move along now!" a rough voice commanded from somewhere in the fog, and the sharp crack of a whip was followed by a scream of pain. "Move along now! You now belong to Emmanuel, and you will do his bidding. Move along now!"

Aldith stared at Gavin, her lips moving wordlessly.

Twenty in all, the line of hapless slaves filed slowly past the confounded travelers. There were men and women in the procession of wretched humanity, and, to Gavin's great dismay, three children. The last slave in line, a skeletal man who looked as if his next breath could be his last, stumbled and fell to his knees as he attempted to step around Gavin. The chains jerked him forward unmercifully, skinning his knees and shins across the rocky trail.

Gavin leaped forward and lifted the man to his feet. "Beware the mountain," the pitiful creature croaked.

Gavin stared at the man. "What?"

"Beware the mountain," the man repeated, and then was pulled forward by the chain. "Beware Thunder Mountain." The swirling mists closed about him, concealing him from view.

Gavin ran through the fog, catching the man's shoulder as if to hold him back. "Wait, sir," he pleaded. "What did you say?" He walked alongside the stumbling slave to keep him in view.

"Beware of Thunder Mountain," the man said again. "Slaves are made there, lad. If only I had never gone to the mountain." The mists closed around the man, and like an apparition from a nightmare, he was gone.

Gavin turned to rejoin his companions and then jumped in fright as a large horse materialized in front of him. He leaped to one side, cringing as he saw the cruel whip in the rider's hand. The man laughed at the expression on Gavin's face. "We didn't frighten you, did we, lad?"

"Sir, who are these people?" Gavin cried. "Where are they going?"

The man laughed. "Just more slaves for His Majesty, King Emmanuel," he replied cheerfully.

"From whence do they come, sir?"

The man stared at Gavin as if he should know the answer. "From Mount Thelema, lad. Where else?" Clucking to his horse, he disappeared in the mists and rain.

Overwhelmed by the horrors he had just witnessed, Gavin ran up the trail. He came upon his travel companions suddenly. Malcolm was standing in the middle of the trail with an expression of pain and disbelief written across his face. Katherine was huddled against a tree with her face hidden in her hands and Aldith was down upon her knees in the wet grass, sobbing as if her heart would break.

"We need—" Gavin began, and his voice broke. He tried again. "We need to find somewhere to shelter from this rain."

Aldith raised a tear-stained face to him. "Who's going to find shelter for those poor slaves?" she demanded.

Gavin stared at her, unable to answer. He struggled to hold back tears of his own.

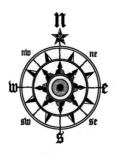

Chapter Sixteen

The sun came out again an hour later and the fog vanished immediately. Once again, the day was bright and cheery and the traveling was pleasant. The four travelers were passing through a forest, and the scent of pine hung heavy in the air. Aldith sniffed the cool mountain breeze. "It smells good, doesn't it?"

The trail wound its way down to a crystal-clear stream and then meandered along its banks. "What if we stop for a brief rest?" Katherine suggested. "Malcolm and I are not as young and energetic as you two." Without waiting for a reply she chose a seat on a large boulder beside the trail. Aldith joined her.

Malcolm and Gavin knelt beside the stream and filled two small flasks with the cool water, which they then offered to the ladies. As Aldith and Katherine were enjoying the refreshing water, the two men knelt and drank directly from the stream. When they had satisfied their thirst they took seats on boulders opposite the ladies.

"We need to talk," Gavin said directly. "There's something we need to discuss before we go another step. I think the same question is going through each of our minds: By traveling to Mount Thelema, are we going into slavery?"

"How could King Emmanuel make slaves of anyone?" Aldith challenged. "We all know that he's too good and too loving for that."

"We all saw the terrible plight of the slaves this morning," Gavin replied. "How do we know that we will not end up in the same condition?"

"What connection is there between Mount Thelema and the slaves we saw?" Malcolm asked.

"When I asked the slave master where the slaves came from, he told me that they were from Mount Thelema!"

The other three travelers were shocked by Gavin's words. "He actually said that?"

"I don't believe that for a minute," Malcolm interjected. "Our King is too kind for that."

"Did you not hear what the last man in line told me?" Gavin asked.

His three companions shook their heads.

"He told me to beware of Thunder Mountain," Gavin told them, "because slaves are made there. As we know, Thunder Mountain is another name for Mount Thelema!"

"I still remember the day when King Emmanuel set me free," Malcolm said, with a faraway look in his eyes. "I was the slave of Argamor, you know, but Emmanuel broke my shackles and set me free! I saw such love in his eyes, such compassion. He loved me as no other has ever loved me. Would he set me free from Argamor just to make me a slave again? Never!"

"Delight told us that the quest for Mount Thelema would bring great joy and sheer delight," Aldith said thoughtfully, "and yet these men on the trail today are warning us to stay away from the mountain. Whom should we believe?"

"The King's book tells us that Emmanuel came to give us abundant life," Malcolm replied. "And that same book is guiding us to the mountain. Make your own choice, but I choose to believe my King!"

"My heart wants to believe my King," Gavin said quietly, "and yet, what if we are walking into a trap? I could not live in chains as those poor souls are living." He shuddered, haunted by the words of the last slave.

The question was on their minds for the rest of the day, and they talked about it from time to time as they journeyed. At last, late in the afternoon, they came to an inn on the outskirts of a small city. "Wouldn't it be lovely if we had money for lodging?" Katherine remarked. "Tonight I could really enjoy the comfort of a featherbed."

Malcolm had his haversack open in a flash and rummaged around in it. His eyes lit up with delight and the others knew that he had found something. "Three silver coins!" he said delightedly, as he drew the money from his pack and held it up with a flourish. "Just the price of a room." He grinned at Aldith and Katherine. "Gavin and I are planning to spend the night here. What about you ladies?"

With a cry of delight, Aldith pulled three coins from her pack. "Our King has provided again," she exulted. "How can we doubt his goodness?"

Katherine displayed several coins. "Unless I'm mistaken, here's the price of dinner for all of us."

"I'll get our rooms," Gavin told Malcolm. "Why don't you take the ladies into the dining room and order dinner?"

As Gavin entered the front room of the inn, he stepped aside for a well-dressed patron, a nobleman, who was just leaving. "Pardon me, sire," Gavin said politely.

The nobleman glanced at Gavin and turned away, and then his mouth actually fell open. "Gavin?" he said in astonishment. "Gavin, the minstrel with the golden voice?"

Gavin nodded. "The same, sire. And where do I know you from, sire?"

"I am Lord Welson. You performed at my castle in North Terrestria a year or two ago, lad. My court has talked about it ever since. You were a sensation!"

The youth smiled modestly. "I'm glad you enjoyed it, sire."

Lord Welson's eyes widened as a sudden thought occurred to him. "Gavin, tell me that you can help me with a problem."

"If I can, sire. How may I be of assistance?"

"My good friend, Lord Cavender, owns this inn and also the Castle Ravenskill. He has hosted a three-day tournament, and the top archers and jousters from all of Terrestria are in attendance, as well as many of nobility. Alas, Cavendar's minstrel has taken sick, and the troupe of dancers he engaged are not available, so tonight we shall have no entertainment. Cavendar is distressed about it, as he wants the tournament and everything connected with it to be a smashing success."

The man gripped Gavin's arm. "Please tell me that you'll perform for us tonight at the castle! You'll get Lord Cavendar out of a real jam and you'll have my undying gratitude, to say nothing of a sizeable remuneration from Cavendar."

Gavin hesitated.

"Oh, do say that you'll do it," Lord Welson pleaded. "Tonight at dinner there will be nearly four hundred in attendance."

Gavin sighed. "I would love to, sire, but I'm on a quest for Mount Thelema."

"Just tonight," the nobleman insisted. "Say you'll do it just tonight. Surely that won't interfere with your quest, will it?"

"I have no lute," Gavin replied.

"That will not present a problem," the nobleman replied, with a laugh. "Lord Cavendar will get you a dozen to choose from!" He gave Gavin a friendly slap on the shoulder. "Half an hour before sundown? Can I count on you? I'll pick you up in my private coach, right here in front of the inn."

Gavin nodded. "I'll be here."

"I will see to it personally that Lord Cavendar makes it worth your while," Lord Welson said, with a delighted grin. "You will not regret this, I assure you. Good day, Gavin my friend, and thank you!"

Gavin was in good spirits as he joined his friends in the dining salon of the inn. "You won't believe what I am planning to do tonight," he told them.

"You plan to have some supper and get some sleep," Aldith teased. "How unusual!"

"More than that," he told her. "Tonight I will perform for some of the richest, most powerful lords and ladies in all Terrestria!"

Malcolm frowned. "Are you in jest?"

"Not at all," Gavin replied. "I have been invited to play and sing for the contestants in one of the most prestigious tournaments in Terrestria, and for their ladies. Many of the nobility will be in attendance. This will be a golden opportunity for me."

"But you are on a quest for Mount Thelema," Aldith said quietly. "I thought that finding the will of your King was the most important priority now."

"Oh, it is," he assured her. "This is a one-time performance. I just promised that I would do it tonight."

"Be careful, lad," Malcolm warned. "Don't let this sidetrack you from the quest."

"I'm just going to perform at Ravenskill Castle tonight," the young minstrel promised. "Tomorrow we shall continue our quest for Thunder Mountain."

"You called it Thunder Mountain," Aldith pointed out.

"You've always called it Mount Thelema before."

Gavin shrugged. "I don't suppose the name makes much difference. Either way, it's still the same mountain."

Half an hour before sunset, Gavin walked out the front door of the inn to find that a coach was waiting, as promised. The driver opened the door, Gavin took a seat within the empty coach, and they were off. Fifteen minutes later, the coach rattled across the drawbridge of a large, forbidding castle and slowed to a stop inside the barbican.

The door opened immediately and Lord Welson stepped forward to greet the young minstrel. "Gavin, so good of you to come. Believe me when I say that you have bailed us out of a very awkward situation. Follow me—I'll introduce you to Lord Cavendar and he'll help you choose a lute."

Together they entered the great hall and Gavin saw that preparations were being made for an elaborate meal. The tables were set with the finest silver and crystal. Servants and scullions were hurrying here and there, busily attending to preparations for the evening. A heavyset nobleman dressed in bright colors and wearing rings on every finger hurried toward them as they entered. "Ah, then you must be Gavin," the man said in greeting. "Your fame precedes you, lad. Lord Welson tells me that you have a voice without equal. I am Lord Cavendar, and I want you to know that we consider ourselves fortunate to have you here. Thank you for coming on such short notice."

"I am glad to be of service, sire."

"You are in need of a lute, I understand?"

"Aye, sire."

"Luke is my personal attendant. He will show you several from which to choose. Ah, it appears that my guests are starting to arrive, and I must show myself the good host, aye? Please inform Luke if you need anything else."

"Thank you, sire."

Five minutes later, Gavin was busily tuning the lute he had chosen and the great hall was filling with guests. It was to be a festive occasion, and the knights, lords, and ladies were in a merry mood. The knights who were competing in the tournament swaggered about the great hall, impressed with their own importance as they talked with the ladies or bantered back and forth with each other. The great hall was abuzz with excitement as the assembled guests debated the strengths and weaknesses of the various champions and attempted to predict the outcome of the tournament. At last, an attendant rang a silver bell to capture attention and Lord Cavendar ascended the dais at one end of the great hall.

"Welcome, welcome, to Ravenskill Castle," he cried. "I trust that you are enjoying the tournament and that your accommodations are comfortable. My chef and his staff have labored hard and spared no expense in preparing the finest meal in all Terrestria just for your dining pleasure. We are honored that you are here."

The nobleman paused as his gaze swept across the sea of faces before him. "For your dining and listening pleasure, we have gone to great lengths and spared no expense to bring you the finest musician in all Terrestria: Gavin, the minstrel with the golden voice. Some of you will recognize this talented young minstrel, as you have heard him at your own castles. For others, this will be a first-time pleasure."

Lord Cavendar smiled broadly. "My friends, we are delighted that you are in attendance tonight at Ravenskill. Sit back, relax, and dine to your heart's content. If there is anything we can do to make the evening more enjoyable, please do not hesitate to approach me or one of my staff. Let the festivities begin!"

The servants moved in at that moment, pouring drinks and

serving the most delicious-looking food that Gavin had ever seen. Sweeping his fingers lightly across the strings, he began to play a cheerful, lilting melody. His heart raced as he played, for music was his passion and performing was his first love, and it had been some time since he had done either. His fingers flew and the music poured from the strings, rich and warm and exhilarating. He looked up to realize that many of the guests were watching him and listening intently, rather than paying attention to the meal.

He threw back his head and began to sing a ballad, and his rich baritone voice filled the great hall. Conversation ceased as the lords and ladies turned to stare at him with rapture in their eyes. Servants forgot their duties and listened with open mouths. Lord Cavendar listened intently for a moment or two and then leaned back in his chair and closed his eyes as a look of pure bliss spread across his broad face.

It was a moment that Gavin would never forget. Time stood still. The delectable meal was temporarily forgotten as guests and servants alike were swept away by the soothing music. Gavin's fingers flew; his voice soared; his heart was overwhelmed by the expansive response to his playing.

When the song came to an end and the last notes died away, there was a long moment of intense silence. Gavin began to strum a few quiet chords, intending to perform another ballad. Abruptly, spontaneous applause started in one corner of the vast chamber and then spread across the assembly like a firestorm. Thunderous applause swept across the great hall; the rafters rang with the sound. After several prolonged moments, the applause died away and Gavin began to play again.

"When was the last time you heard applause for a minstrel?" one of the lords asked his wife. "This young man is incredible."

"He has a voice like no other," the lady agreed.

Gavin moved easily into another song. The servants, finally remembering their duties, again began to serve the dinner guests and the meal was resumed. Conversation was subdued or nonexistent, as most guests seemed intent on hearing every note from the lute and the voice of the talented young minstrel.

For Gavin, it was a night of glory. Never before had he performed for such an appreciative audience; never before had he received such enthusiastic response. The nobility, the tournament champions, and the castle staff alike applauded eagerly after every number. Lord Cavendar beamed and beamed.

At last, the magical evening came to a close. When the last morsel of food had been consumed and the sweets and confections had been enjoyed, Lord Cavendar rose to his feet. "My friends, this has been an evening to remember. I'm sure you will agree that the food has been exceptional. Your company has been delightful. And no one would disagree when I say that the music this evening has been the finest ever heard in all Terrestria. We have tomorrow evening to look forward to, for I am pleased to announce that this golden-voiced minstrel will be with us again at dinner. I will make sure of that."

At these words, the crowd of delighted dinner guests rose to their feet, cheering and applauding enthusiastically. The great hall rang with the sound. The young minstrel stood on the dais, overwhelmed by the enthusiastic response.

Twenty minutes later, Lord Cavendar himself accompanied Gavin on the coach ride back to the inn. "You were phenomenal, sir," the exuberant nobleman told him. "My guests loved you! We cannot wait for tomorrow night!"

"Sire," Gavin interrupted, "I cannot perform tomorrow night, for I am on a quest to Mount Thelema. My companions and I must leave tomorrow morning at first light."

"Oh, but you must perform," the heavyset host insisted. "My guests are already planning on it."

"But, sire, I cannot—" Gavin protested, but Lord Cavendar grabbed his hand and dropped a handful of golden coins into it.

"Tomorrow night will be twice as much," he promised.

Gavin stared at the money. "Sire, this is more—"

"Don't worry about it," the nobleman said with a laugh and a wave of his hand. "You were worth every bit of that and more. My guests will talk of this evening for years to come. Lord Welson was right—you are the most phenomenal minstrel that either of us has ever heard!"

The coach wheel bumped over a rut just then, causing Gavin to drop some of the money. He bent over to pick it up. "Sire, I appreciate your generosity, but I cannot perform—"

"Of course you'll be there, Gavin," Lord Cavendar interrupted. "I have told my guests that you will be performing, and we cannot go back on our word, can we now?"

"No, sire, but—"

"Then it's settled," the enthusiastic man declared. "My carriage will pick you up at the inn tomorrow evening at the very same time." He glanced at the golden coins in Gavin's hands. "None of that goes for your food or lodging, Gavin. I own the inn, and the accommodations for you and your friends are already provided."

"You're going to do what?" Malcolm stared at Gavin. "Are you forgetting that we are on a quest for Mount Thelema? We agreed that the quest was priority—nothing would divert or distract us from reaching the sacred mountain."

"But I can't help it," Gavin replied miserably. He looked

helplessly from one of his friends to the others. All three had stayed up to meet him when he returned from his performance at Ravenskill Castle. "Lord Cavendar already told his dinner guests that I would be returning tomorrow night. They gave me a standing ovation when he announced it."

Aldith gave him a look of admiration. "You must be really good."

Gavin shrugged.

"But how can you do this to us?" Katherine demanded. "We will have to wait here for an entire day just so that you can perform tomorrow night at the castle. We'll miss a whole day of travel!"

"Go without me," Gavin replied.

"You know we can't do that," Malcolm said quietly. "We're in this together."

"I'll hire a carriage and catch up to you," Gavin replied. "Lord Cavendar paid me enough to hire five coaches, and he promised me twice as much tomorrow."

"So this is about money?" Aldith asked, with a look of bitter disappointment in her eyes.

"Nay," Gavin retorted. "Lord Cavendar told the people I would be there! I can't make him go back on his word."

"Will you promise us that after tomorrow night you will not perform again at the castle?" Katherine asked.

Gavin sighed. "I'm only going back one more night."

"Then promise us. We'll wait here tomorrow, and then leave at first light the next day."

Gavin squirmed.

Aldith studied his face. "It's more than just the money. What happened tonight?"

Gavin's eyes lit up at the memory. "This audience was like no other that I have ever played for. They listened intently to every song; they applauded after every selection. They were the most responsive group that I have ever performed for! Sometimes in the middle of a song I would look out and see ladies in tears. I saw men who forgot to eat because they were so caught up in my music. Do you know what that means to a minstrel? A man could live a hundred years and never again play before an audience like that. I—I have to perform again tomorrow!"

Malcolm sighed and looked at Katherine and Aldith. "Ladies, I hate to say this, but I'm afraid that soon there will only be three of us on the quest for Mount Thelema."

"Don't say that!" Gavin begged. "I'm still with you on this quest. I just want one more night."

"Beware that a second night at the castle doesn't lead to a third and a fourth," Aldith said quietly.

A strange light appeared in Gavin's eyes. "If King Emmanuel gave me this talent, should I not use it? Would it not be wrong to simply set my music aside, since the ability was given to me by my King?"

"He wants you to use it for his glory and for his kingdom," Aldith replied. "From what you told us, tonight you did neither."

"I'll just perform one more night," Gavin promised. "Then we'll all resume the quest together. My music shall not keep me from Mount Thelema."

"We'll see," Malcolm replied. The words were a challenge.

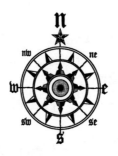

Chapter Seventeen

The moon hung low in the heavens, a huge silver medallion shining so brightly that the walls of Ravenskill Castle gleamed like polished silver. A gentle wind stirred in the treetops, rustling the leaves and sweeping cool air across the face of Terrestria. A stately coach made its way down the narrow lane leading from the castle. Inside the magnificent carriage, a young minstrel leaned back comfortably in the cushions and relived the events of the evening.

Just as they had the night before, the residents, guests, and servants at Ravenskill had responded eagerly to Gavin's music. The young minstrel had been in top form, powerful and witty in his stage presence, playing the lute flawlessly, his golden voice rendering each song so fully and convincingly that more than once the audience was moved to tears. The applause had been deafening; the accolades and compliments flattering but sincere. As the coach rolled smoothly along, Gavin found himself looking forward to the next night's performance.

There was only one cloud on Gavin's horizon. Unable to resist a third invitation, he had broken the promises he had made to his travel companions, and he knew what Malcolm and the others would say about that. He was not looking forward to the reception at the inn.

The coach slowed and the voice of the driver interrupted his thoughts. "There seems to be an old man in the roadway ahead, sir. Shall we stop?"

"Certainly," Gavin replied. "Perhaps someone needs our assistance."

The coach rolled to a smooth stop, and Gavin heard the driver call out, "May we be of service, sir? Do you need help?"

Moments later, the door of the carriage opened and the driver appeared in the doorway, accompanied by an elderly man. "Begging pardon, sir," the driver addressed Gavin, "but I saw fit to give this gentleman a ride, but only if it pleases you, sir."

"It's fine," Gavin replied, watching as the old man took a seat with head bowed. The door closed, and moments later the carriage started forward. The old man lifted his head and looked at Gavin, and the young minstrel stared in utter amazement. "Sir Wisdom!"

"So now we're riding in luxurious carriages rather than striving to reach Mount Thelema," the old nobleman said with a mournful shake of the head. "So tell me, Gavin, how went the performance at Ravenskill Castle? This was your second night there, I believe?"

Gavin found that somehow he couldn't meet the old man's gaze. "It—it went fine, sire."

"And you're scheduled for a third appearance tomorrow night, am I right?" Sir Wisdom said reprovingly. "Though, of course, that means that you are willing to break certain promises to your companions on the quest."

"Lord Cavendar pressed me," Gavin blurted, "and I couldn't refuse him."

"Was it the money, or the prestige?"

Gavin stared at him. "Sire?"

"What compelled you to break your promises—the money you would earn or the prestige that you would enjoy?"

Gavin was silent.

"Oh, Gavin, can't you see what the adversary is doing? Argamor is diverting you from your quest to Mount Thelema, for he would keep you from finding and doing the will of your King. He caused you to doubt Emmanuel's love and goodness toward you by leading you to believe that yielding to Emmanuel will enslave you. You are becoming fearful of Mount Thelema, for deep in your heart you are fearful of becoming a slave. Argamor has also diverted you from your quest by capitalizing on the musical talent that His Majesty has given you and persuading you to use it for your own honor and glory."

The young minstrel hung his head. "How do you know these things, sire?"

"Your companions are also struggling, for Argamor is seeking to divert them as well. You should know that your decision will affect them greatly. As you know, for a time Malcolm was fearful and unsure about the quest, though you were a help to him and he now trusts his King. Aldith is uncertain, and she is looking to you for leadership. If you were to abandon the quest, almost immediately she would too. And Katherine—well, you have more influence on Katherine than you realize. You're a leader, Gavin, a natural leader with a strong personality. That's one reason you enjoy performing: you enjoy influencing others. Again, you should know that any decision you make will strongly impact Malcolm, Aldith, and Katherine."

"I did not realize that I had that much influence on them."

"Aye, lad, you do."

Gavin was quiet and thoughtful for a moment. "How do I know that the quest to Mount Thelema will not enslave us?"

BOOK ONE: TALES FROM TERRESTRIA

The old man looked deeply into his eyes. "Do you honestly believe for one moment that King Emmanuel could find it in his gentle, loving heart to enslave you? Surely you know your King better than that!"

"What about the slaves we saw yesterday?" Gavin demanded in an attempt to defend himself. "The slave master told me that those poor wretches were coming from Mount Thelema."

"And you believed him rather than trusting your King."

"Do you know what the last slave on the chain told me? He said that he became a slave by going to Mount Thelema."

"Gavin, Gavin." Sir Wisdom shook his head sadly. "Argamor has put together an elaborate charade and you have fallen for it. The men and women you saw on the slave line were not slaves to Emmanuel, for His Majesty owns no slaves. Those poor souls were, instead, slaves to none other than Argamor."

"Are you certain, sire?"

"Absolutely."

"I didn't know," Gavin said feebly.

"And now you are entertaining each night at Ravenskill Castle rather than finishing the quest for Mount Thelema. 'No man, having put his hand to the plow, and looking back, is fit for the kingdom.'"

"Did not Emmanuel himself give me this skill?" Gavin argued. "Is it wrong to make use of it?"

"It is wrong to use it for yourself, as you are now doing," the old man replied. "Lad, you were given your great musical talent to glorify your King. Use it to honor Emmanuel, not yourself."

"What am I to do, sire?" Gavin said at last. "I have given Lord Cavendar my word that I will perform."

"You also gave your word to Aldith, Katherine, and Malcolm that you would not perform a third night."

Gavin hung his head.

Sir Wisdom was thoughtful for a moment. "Go to your travel companions and beg their forgiveness," he said at last. "Give one final performance at Ravenskill, but don't sing ballads and love songs; instead sing music that glorifies Emmanuel. And be sure to tell Lord Cavendar immediately that this is your final performance."

The young minstrel hesitated.

"Gavin, you need to decide once and for all what you are going to do," Sir Wisdom said sternly. "You cannot serve your King and serve yourself at the same time. It's one or the other, sir. If the praise of men means more to you than the praise of your King, then stay here and continue to entertain the folks at Ravenskill, but in doing so, you will have to abandon the quest for Mount Thelema. If you truly desire to find the will of your King, then you have to be willing to give up your life as a minstrel."

"Does King Emmanuel not want me to be a minstrel?"

"I didn't say that, Gavin, for I do not know his plan for you. But any man who is truly desirous of learning the will of the King must be willing to forsake all to follow him. In your case, that means being willing to give up the life of a minstrel."

"But did not His Majesty give me this ability? Should I not use it?"

"'Tis true, your ability did come from Emmanuel, but you must be willing to surrender it to him and use it only for his glory."

"What if I get to Mount Thelema and find that His Majesty wants me to give up the life of a minstrel entirely? Music is my passion, sire, and performing is my love. I enjoy performing for others as I enjoy nothing else. I—I do not know that I could give it up."

"Do you love performing more than you love your King?"

"In truth, I do not know, sire. I would hope that my love for Emmanuel is greater than my love for anything else, but I do not know."

"Would you give it up if His Majesty asked you to do so?"

Gavin sighed. "What if I get to Mount Thelema and find that His Majesty wants something for me that I just cannot bear? What if he wants me to give up my performing and I find that I just cannot do that?"

"Can you not leave the choice with your King and trust him to plan what's best for you? Emmanuel knows what is best for you, lad, and if you leave the choice to him, he will give you what is best. Many times we seek our own happiness rather than seeking to please the King and we miss out on the life of joy and fulfillment that he has planned for us."

Gavin stared at him. "When we were in the City-That-Was-Never-Built, Desire said the very same thing. She said that Emmanuel's children miss the Banquet of Joy because they scramble for the scraps and crumbs of their own happiness, rather than yielding to the will of their King and enjoying his bounty!"

"She said it well." The old man studied the face of the young minstrel. "Oh, Gavin, you must decide. Will you seek the King's will, yielding yourself whole-heartedly to it and therefore enjoy the Banquet of Joy that comes from a yielded heart, or will you seek your own plans and therefore exist on scraps and crumbs? The choice is yours, lad, for His Majesty will not force you to yield."

Gavin sighed. "This is not an easy decision, sire."

"I know it's not. I was not present for your performances at Ravenskill Castle, and yet I know that the response you received from the people was very gratifying. Humans thrive on praise, and it's always fulfilling to know that your efforts are appreciated. Applause and adulation is heady stuff. Now that you have received such a thrilling reception from the residents of Ravenskill, you will find yourself wanting more and more and you will find it very difficult to give it up. But remember, Gavin, your King always gives his very best to those who seek his will and allow him to make their decisions."

Gavin was silent for several long moments and the old nobleman waited patiently, realizing that the decision was Gavin's and that it must come from his heart.

"I want Emmanuel's will for my life," Gavin said finally, "and yet I find myself wanting my own way also. I enjoy performing, enjoy it immensely, and I suppose that I am afraid that if I yield to Emmanuel's will, it will mean giving up performing forever. Oh, Sir Wisdom, it is as though I am being torn in two!"

"There is yet one other matter that you must consider as you make your decision," Sir Wisdom said quietly.

"What is that, sire?"

"King Emmanuel is the one who set you free from slavery. But for him, you would still wear the chain of iniquity and be the slave of Argamor."

Gavin nodded. "Aye."

"And you know the price that Emmanuel paid to set you free: he gave his life for you. He died that you might be free. Gavin, your life is not your own, for you were bought with a tremendous price."

The coach slowed, and both knew that they were nearing the inn. "What will you do, Gavin?"

"I—I must know and do the will of my King, sire. I will continue on the quest for Mount Thelema, for I must please the one who died for me. If Emmanuel's plan for me means giving up performing, then I shall give up performing."

Gavin kept his word. After explaining the matter to Malcolm, Aldith, and Katherine and seeking their forgiveness, he went the next night to Ravenskill Castle for a third and final performance. Just as before, the reception from the crowd assembled in the great hall was more than enthusiastic. As he played and sang, Gavin's heart was heavy, for he knew that this would be his last performance. And yet, there was a calm and settled peace within his heart, for his music that night honored the King and he knew that he was making the right decision.

Lord Cavendar found him after the performance. "Excellent, Gavin, just excellent, as usual. Your performances have made this tournament an event to be remembered. My guests have talked more about your music than they have about the tournament itself. The competitions during the day have been insignificant compared with your performances each evening."

Gavin nodded humbly. "I thank you, sire."

The nobleman placed a small bag of gold coins in his hand. "I have a proposition for you—I want you to take a regular position here at Ravenskill. You will be my personal attendant during the day and the castle minstrel each evening. I will pay you wages far greater than any other minstrel in Terrestria."

Gavin hesitated for just a moment and then slowly shook his head. "Thank you, sire, for I am grateful for your confidence in me, and yet I cannot accept. I must continue on my quest for Mount Thelema. I must find and do the will of my King."

"You had better think it through, lad. This is an offer that most musicians would jump at. Ravenskill is one of the most prestigious castles in all Terrestria, and you will regularly perform before some of the greatest names in the kingdom. Your wages will be many times greater than any other minstrel has ever made. Don't say nay too quickly."

"My mind is made up, sire. My companions and I will leave for Mount Thelema at first light tomorrow morning."

Lord Cavendar's face grew dark with displeasure. "You are making a mistake."

"I have thought it through, sire, and I must do the will of my King."

For some unexplained reason, Lord Cavendar's carriage was not available that evening and Gavin found himself walking back to the inn in the darkness.

Early the next morning, the four travelers set off once again for Mount Thelema. They left the inn in high spirits. "It is good to be on the road to the sacred mountain again, is it not?" Aldith commented, as they hurried down the busy main street of the little city. "I wonder how far it is now to the mountain?"

"There is no way to know, I suppose," Malcolm replied. "It is simply our duty to keep traveling until we reach it."

"Let us covenant with each other not to stop until we reach the mountain," Katherine suggested. "Let nothing distract or discourage us from finding the will of our King."

"I am sorry for the delay that I have caused these last two days," Gavin said contritely. "It is entirely my fault that we have been delayed."

"You have been forgiven," Malcolm replied. "Let us leave this incident in the past and press forward until we complete our quest and learn the will of our King."

The four travelers passed through the gate and left the

city behind them. They found themselves traveling through a pleasant valley with gentle, rolling hills on each side. An occasional farm dotted the landscape. Less than two furlongs from the city, they came to a fork in the road. "Let me check the book," Gavin told the others.

He opened his book and noted that the pages glowed brightly when he turned the book to the east, but dimmed when turned facing to the north. "The road to the east it is, then," he said aloud.

"The road to the east travels through a dark and lonely canyon," Aldith said, pointing, "while the road to the north travels through a wide, pleasant valley. Perhaps we should take the road to the north."

Malcolm checked his own book. "The path that we should follow is not always the easiest one," he told Aldith. "Gavin is right—we must take the road to the east."

The four travelers took the road to the east and within two or three furlongs they entered a steep canyon. The road narrowed and became little more than a footpath, winding its way upward and becoming steeper by the minute. The canyon was dark and gloomy and reeked of rotting vegetation.

"I don't like this place," Aldith remarked as she looked about fearfully. "It looks so dark and...dangerous."

At that moment, a man came dashing down the trail toward them, running as if his life were in jeopardy. His eyes were wide and his face was filled with terror. "Run for your lives!" he cried as he ran past. "A horrible dragon is upon us!"

Chapter Eighteen

Gavin and his companions stared at the frightened stranger as he ran recklessly down the narrow canyon. As they watched, he missed his footing and fell headlong on the rocky trail, skinning his hands and knees. He leaped to his feet and ran on.

"He acted as if he was absolutely terrified," Aldith commented. "Are we in danger?"

Gavin glanced down at the open volume in his hands. "My book says that this is the way," he replied, "so this is the route that Emmanuel has planned for us. If we are indeed following his leading, we are in perfect safety and will come to no harm, though we—"

At that moment, an ear-splitting roar resounded through the canyon, echoing and re-echoing and growing louder and louder until the four travelers covered their ears in pain. "Run!" Gavin shouted. "Run for your lives!"

Gavin and his companions dashed down the narrow trail. Another prolonged roar of rage sounded in the canyon behind them, urging them to greater speed. "The dragon is after us!" Aldith cried. "Where shall we go?"

"To the city!" Katherine answered. In spite of her age and her weight she passed the others and took the lead.

In moments the gates of the city came into view and the four travelers ran for them as fast as they could go. Hearts pounding with fear, they dashed through the gates and then sighed with relief as they realized that they were safe. They had escaped the dragon. Sides heaving, they panted as they struggled to catch their breath.

"Escaped the dragon, did you?" a voice called, and Gavin looked up to see the stranger that they had encountered in the canyon. The man seemed almost amused as he asked, "Whatever were you doing in the Valley of Dragons?"

"The Valley of Dragons, sir?" Malcolm responded. "Pray tell, is there more than one dragon?"

"The Valley of Dragons is home to at least a dozen dragons, perhaps more," another voice replied, and the four travelers realized that a small crowd was gathering. The speaker was an older man with a wizened face and a long beard.

"Only a fool would venture into the Valley of Dragons without a compelling reason," the first stranger told them. "It is a place of extreme danger."

"Why then did you go in, sir?" Malcolm challenged.

The stranger sighed. "My best milk cow wandered into the valley this morning," he said, with a regretful shake of the head. "She is a valuable animal, sir, or I wouldn't have taken the risk. Alas, one of the dragons came before I could find my cow. You know the rest."

"What do the dragons look like?" Aldith asked, gazing about at the crowd of townspeople who had gathered. "How big are they?"

"We do not know, my lady," a thin-faced woman answered, "for not one of us has ever seen one."

"Nobody has ever seen one of the dragons?" Katherine was incredulous. "Then how do you know that they exist?"

"We have seen their shadows and we have heard their roaring," a man replied, "but we have never seen one face to face." He shrugged. "And believe me, that is for the best!"

"Shadows never hurt anyone," Malcolm said quietly.

"My foolish friend," one man replied impatiently, "where there are shadows of dragons, there are dragons. The shadows do not create themselves."

The cobbler started to reply but then closed his mouth and said nothing.

"We are traveling to Mount Thelema," Gavin told the people, "and the King's book says that we must follow the trail through the Valley of Dragons. Is there another way?"

"Mount Thelema?" the first stranger echoed. "You would go to Thunder Mountain, my lord?"

"Aye. We are seeking the will of King Emmanuel."

The man shook his head. "I have never been to Thunder Mountain, my lord, but I have heard that it is a place of danger. It is a place of thunder and lightning, a place of death and sorrow, a place where free men become slaves. Wherefore would you go to Thunder Mountain, sir?"

"We seek the sacred mountain that we might find the will of our King. Is there another route that we might take to the mountain, rather than passing through the Valley of Dragons?"

"The Valley of Dragons is the only way," several townspeople muttered at once. "That is why we have never gone to the mountain."

"Tell us about the dragons," Malcolm requested. "How many are there? How big are they? Do you know of anyone who has killed one?"

"Stranger, your questions tell me that you are thinking of venturing back into the Valley of Dragons," a tall man said. "Only a fool would do that."

"If the Valley of Dragons is the only way to Mount Thelema," Malcolm answered evenly, "then my friends and I must traverse the valley, for we will find the sacred mountain or die."

"Then die you will, my friend. The dragons will see to that."

The townspeople laughed.

"Turn back, my friends," an old woman advised. "We do not wish to hear of your deaths." The entire crowd nodded and agreed with the woman.

"We will not be dissuaded from our quest," Gavin declared. "Even if we must face a score of dragons, we must go to the mountain." Malcolm, Katherine, and Aldith all voiced their assent.

"Then this is good-bye, my friends, for we will not see you again," the woman said sadly. The townspeople all nodded and sighed with grief.

Gavin looked to his companions. "Are we in agreement? Do we go back to the Valley of Dragons and face whatever comes?"

"We're with you, lad," Malcolm said. Katherine and Aldith nodded.

"Then let us be off." Gavin raised his voice. "Thank you for your kind words of advice, my friends, and thank you for your concern for our safety. In spite of your words of warning, we must pass through this valley of danger, for we are following the guidance of our King. We will find the sacred mountain."

The four travelers hurried back through the city gates and started again for the forbidding canyon. Gavin pointed to a shady spot beneath four giant oaks. "Let us pause in this beautiful glen and seek Emmanuel's protection. Let us read from Emmanuel's book and send petitions to the Golden City. If we are indeed in a place of danger, we dare not go without his protection and guidance."

Gavin and his companions spent a quiet interlude in the peaceful glen, each reading the King's book and sending petitions seeking protection from the dragons. Just before leaving the glen, they paused as a group to sing a song of praise to Emmanuel.

"Draw your swords," Gavin instructed, "for we know not yet what dangers we face from the dragons."

They entered the canyon with swords drawn, walking as quietly as possible, though each sound they made was amplified many times within the canyon. The canyon walls were almost perpendicular at that point, chalky white in appearance and soaring high above their heads like the battlements of a castle. "I see no sign of a dragon," Malcolm said, and his voice boomed like the roar of thunder.

"There is no need to shout," Gavin replied, irritated, "for we are right beside—" He stopped, confused, for he had spoken softly, yet his voice came booming back at him as loud as Malcolm's.

Malcolm and Gavin looked at each other in bewilderment.

"The canyon walls increase the sound," Katherine whispered softly, but her words could have been heard half a mile away. "Each sound we make is amplified a thousand times!"

"I still see no sign of a dragon," Malcolm whispered. "Perhaps there is no danger here, after all."

Like a crash of thunder, a mighty roar rocked the canyon just then, shaking the rocks and causing tiny stones to tumble down upon the four travelers. Completely unnerved, Malcolm, Aldith, and Katherine turned to flee. "Wait!" Gavin cried. "Perhaps there is no danger upon us."

Aldith trembled as she pointed at the chalky canyon wall behind Gavin. "Th-then w-what is th-that?"

Gavin turned, and his heart seemed to stop. The rising

sun shone directly on the canyon wall, illuminating it so that it seemed to glow. Just above Gavin on the chalky wall was the dark form of an enormous dragon. The massive head was thrown back; the mouth was open in a snarl of rage; the front claws opened and closed threateningly. The mighty tail whipped back and forth like the tail of an enormous serpent.

"It—it's a dragon!" Katherine whispered in terror.

Another roar of rage shook the canyon from one end to the other.

"It's just a shadow," Malcolm replied.

"But where there are shadows of dragons, there are dragons," Aldith replied fearfully, as she quickly scanned the canyon. "But where can it be? I do not see it."

The dragon roared again, a prolonged outburst of fury that caused the trees to tremble and the rocks to quake. A tremor ran through the rocky floor beneath the feet of the travelers. White with terror, Aldith covered her ears with her hands. Fear shot through the travelers like bolts of lightning, but they stood their ground.

"What is that?" Katherine cried, pointing.

Her three companions turned. Perched atop a rock formation in the center of the canyon was a fierce-looking creature with grayish-green scales covering most of its hideous body. Sharp spikes protected its head and throat and ran the length of its back and tail. The beast's mouth was wide open and it hissed and snarled, violently thrashing its long, spiked tail from side to side. Rising up on its hind legs, it reached for them, opening and closing its claws as if anxious to tear them limb from limb.

"What is it?" Katherine asked again. Mystified, she moved closer, as did her companions.

"It's just a lizard," Gavin said, laughing with relief. "Our dragon is nothing but a lizard!"

"Whoever saw a lizard this big?" Aldith replied. "It's nearly four feet long. Maybe it's a young dragon!"

"If so, then the mother dragon may be sixty feet long and lurking somewhere nearby," Katherine said, looking about the canyon anxiously. "Let's get out of here."

"We're quite safe," Malcolm told them, laughing. "Actually, this fierce-looking creature is just a harmless lizard. It's called an iguana. I once saw one when I was on a trip to South Terrestria."

Gavin turned and glanced at the enormous shadow on the canyon wall. "The morning sun comes through that pass to the east at just the right angle to throw the lizard's shadow on the wall," he observed.

"Magnifying it and making it look huge," Aldith finished for him.

"And the echoes in the canyon amplify the creature's hissing and snarling a thousand times, creating the roar of a dragon," Katherine commented. "The townspeople have been terrified of a harmless lizard!"

"Aye, but a rather big lizard," Aldith replied, with a laugh. "And it is quite ferocious-looking."

"I rather suspect that most of our fears and worries in this life are as groundless as the terrors in the Valley of Dragons," Malcolm said, with a wry smile. "How often we look at shadows on the wall instead of trusting the promises of our mighty King."

"How many times must we learn to trust Emmanuel," Gavin agreed. "It seems that is a lesson that I have to learn again and again."

"Don't we all?" Katherine remarked.

Malcolm stepped closer and extended his sword toward the

hissing iguana. The creature snarled and snapped at the weapon, but as Malcolm continued to poke at it, the lizard abruptly turned and dashed out of sight behind the rock.

"Shall we tell the townsfolk that their dragon is nothing but a harmless lizard?" Aldith asked.

"It would do no good," Katherine replied. "They would never believe us."

"Shall we continue?" Gavin suggested. "On to Mount Thelema!"

"On to Mount Thelema," his companions chorused.

An hour later, the canyon came to an abrupt end, opening out on a wide, grassy plain. As they emerged from the canyon, Malcolm pointed to the north. "Look! Mount Thelema!"

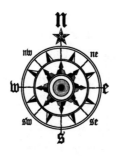

Chapter Nineteen

The four travelers stood in stunned silence, overwhelmed at their first sight of the sacred mountain.

Far in the distance, Mount Thelema stood before them, enormous, dark, and forbidding, almost sinister in appearance. Dark, thick clouds shrouded the mountain, obscuring the peaks. As they gazed upon the object of their quest, jagged bolts of lightning shot from the clouds to strike the ridges. Thunder rumbled ominously.

"Thunder Mountain," Gavin said quietly, and a feeling of elation swept over him; and yet, at the same time, he felt an overriding sense of fear. "We've reached our destination."

"It's so dark," Aldith remarked. "It looks frightening—almost like an enormous enemy castle."

"The dark cleft in the middle does resemble the entrance to a castle, does it not?" Malcolm commented.

"We cannot even see how tall it is," Katherine said, "for the clouds obscure the peaks. It could take days and days to climb to the top."

The clouds encircling the mountain surged and swirled, continuously moving and changing shape, shrouding the peaks as though they were guarding some forbidden secret. Lightning flashed repeatedly, lighting the clouds from within and giving the mountain an eerie, otherworldly appearance. Thunder growled as if to warn away any who would venture too close.

Gavin took a deep breath. "Well, we're almost to the mountain," he said, and his voice cracked with apprehension. "Shall we pause and send petitions?"

Following his suggestion, the travelers took parchments from within their books and wrote petitions to King Emmanuel. Gavin wrote:

> "My Lord, King Emmanuel,
> We thank you for your protection and guidance on our quest for Mount Thelema. We now have the mountain in sight, my Lord, and yet must confess that we are experiencing fears and misgivings. Guide us, we ask, and protect us as we climb the mountain. We long to know and do your will.
> Your son, Gavin."

The young minstrel rolled the document tightly and released it. He watched as the petition soared from his hand and shot over the mountains in a thin streak of silver light. Moments later, similar streaks of light shot across the skies as the others sent petitions.

"Well," Malcolm said, as he replaced his book within his doublet, "we have a long trek ahead of us if we intend to reach the base of the mountain before nightfall. Shall we get started?"

Aldith looked at him in surprise. "How far away do you think the mountain is?"

The cobbler shrugged as he studied the vast plain before them. "Maybe twenty-five or thirty miles?"

"Twenty-five or thirty miles!" The girl was astounded. "I thought it was just a mile or two."

Malcolm shook his head. "Distances can be deceiving. I

think you'll be amazed at just how enormous this mountain really is, once we get close. Right now, I'd say we're at least twenty-five miles from it."

Gavin took off his haversack and started rummaging through it. "There won't be any water out on this plain. If we have a trek of twenty-five or thirty miles ahead of us, I wonder if we'll have enough food and water to last through the day."

"Gavin, Gavin," Malcolm said reprovingly, "we have seen our King provide our every need so far. Why would he fail us now?"

Gavin nodded meekly as he reclosed the pack. "There was food and water."

"You were looking at the shadows on the wall," Aldith said gently, "instead of trusting the promises of our King."

The young minstrel smiled meekly. "Aye, as I said when we saw the iguana, trusting the King is a lesson that I seem to have to learn again and again." He glanced up at the thundering mountain. "Well, we're off to Mount Thelema!"

The four travelers started across the plain, always keeping the sacred mountain directly in front of them. After fifteen minutes of walking, Aldith gave a long sigh. "It doesn't look like we're getting any closer."

Malcolm laughed. "We've got a long way to go, lass. We'll walk quite a distance before you can tell that we're getting any closer."

Aldith caught up with Gavin and began to walk alongside him. "I can hardly wait to learn of Emmanuel's plans for me!" She turned to face him. "If you could choose your own destiny and be anything you wanted, what would you choose?"

Gavin thought about it for the briefest instant before replying. "I love music and I love performing. If I could choose, I suppose that I would choose the life of a minstrel again. But as you know, Aldith, I gave that up to seek the will of Emmanuel. My heart is yielded, so anything that His Majesty chooses is fine with me."

She studied his face. "Do you really mean that?"

He nodded. "If I know my heart, I do."

The girl looked at Malcolm. "What would you choose, sir?"

Malcolm was thoughtful. "I enjoyed my life as a cobbler, but as Gavin just said, I want my King to choose for me. If I have learned one thing on this quest, I have learned that I can trust my King. I know he will choose what's best for me, so whatever his will involves, I will delight in it."

He looked at her intently. "What would you choose?"

Aldith smiled shyly. "I think my heart is yielded, and I will find delight in whatever Emmanuel chooses for me, but I would simply like to be a wife and mother. One day I want to have a home and have children to call my own."

Gavin's heart pounded. *What a beautiful wife you will make and what a sweet mother you would be,* he thought wistfully. *How fortunate the man whom the King chooses as your husband.*

Malcolm looked at Katherine. "And what would you choose, my lady?"

Katherine shrugged. "As you know, I come from a long line of nobility. I have enjoyed a life of wealth, privilege, and status. Whatever Emmanuel chooses for me is fine, as long as it befits a lady of my standing."

"But what if Emmanuel should choose something less than that?" Aldith inquired. "Remember what Delight told us in the City-That-Was-Never-Built? She said that there are no titles of nobility in the family of King Emmanuel."

Katherine didn't answer.

The trek across the vast, grassy plains took hours and hours. The four travelers kept their eyes on Mount Thelema as they walked, but the thundering mountain just didn't seem to get any closer. At last, Katherine called for a break. "Let's find a place to sit and rest, shall we?" she begged. "I'm tired and I'm mighty hungry."

"There's a grove of trees just two or three furlongs ahead," Gavin said, spotting a clump of acacia trees that jutted like an island in the vast sea of grass. "Perhaps there is a spring there so that we may bathe our weary feet. Can you walk that far?"

The woman nodded wearily. "Aye. The shade alone is worth waiting for."

Within minutes they reached the grove and found a spring bubbling up from the ground, cool and clear and inviting. Seated on an outcropping of pure white limestone was an old man with a friendly smile. Gavin was astonished. "Sir Wisdom!"

The old man stood and lifted his hands toward them. "Welcome, weary ones, welcome! Pause and rest and bathe your weary feet. Your quest has gone well and you are to be commended for your steadfastness. Many a son or daughter of the King would have turned back in discouragement and defeat long ago, yet you have stayed faithful to the quest. His Majesty is proud of your great accomplishments on this treacherous journey to the thundering mountain."

The four travelers sat on the bank of the inviting spring and removed their shoes. With luxurious sighs of relief they plunged their feet into the cool, swirling waters. "Ah," Gavin sighed. "My feet were ready for this!" He looked at the old man. "How much farther to Mount Thelema?"

The old man grinned broadly. "Do I have good news for you! King Emmanuel has decreed that you do not have to climb to the top of the sacred mountain to learn his will. You have showed your faithfulness on this quest and he has rewarded you accordingly." With a flourish, he pulled four rolled parchments from within his cloak. "Behold! The decreed will of the King for each of you. All that His Majesty would ask is that you not open these until you have made your way back to your homes."

Gavin felt like shouting. "We do not have to go all the way to Mount Thelema? Feet of mine, rejoice!"

Aldith laughed. "My weary feet are delighted with the news, I'm sure."

Malcolm was skeptical. "Emmanuel has decided that we no longer have to go all the way to the mountain? But why would he change his mind?"

"Oh, he has not changed his mind," the old man replied grandly. "He is simply rewarding you for your courage and faithfulness in making the journey. The quest for the thundering mountain was simply a test, and you have passed the test."

"Well, I for one am delighted with this bit of good news," Katherine declared, and her companions laughed, for they knew how she detested walking. "We thank you, Sir Wisdom, for delivering this reprieve."

The old man smiled and nodded. "I am delighted to be at your service." He began to pass the rolled parchments to each of the four travelers, studying the seal on each before handing it to the proper person. Each of the four was delighted upon receiving the parchment and thanked the old man profusely.

Unnoticed by any of the four, a snowy white dove flew from tree to tree, anxiously calling in a quiet voice that was easily ignored.

After a quick lunch in the peaceful glen, Malcolm, Gavin, Aldith, and Katherine repacked their things, thanked the old man again, and started back across the vast grassy plain. Gavin studied the rolled parchment in his hand. "I am anxious to get back and open this roll," he said excitedly, "that I might learn the will of my King. I only wish that I could open it now."

Aldith opened her book, studied it for a moment, and then cried out in dismay, "Wait! Wait! I fear that we are going the wrong way!"

"Going the wrong way?" Gavin echoed. "How could we be going the wrong way? Did not King Emmanuel send us back this way?"

The girl turned her book from one side to another. "The book says to continue to Mount Thelema," she told the others. "What can this mean?"

Gavin opened his own book and quickly checked it. "Mine also directs me toward Mount Thelema," he reported. He frowned in bewilderment. "But Sir Wisdom told us that we were to go back home. Why would Emmanuel order us back home if his book directs us to go on to the sacred mountain?"

"The King's book is never wrong," Malcolm declared emphatically. "Of this I am certain. We can trust the book to always lead us in the right path."

"But Sir Wisdom told us that King Emmanuel wants us to go back home," Gavin argued.

The cobbler shook his head. "I will follow the book. We do not know for certain that His Majesty has ordered us to return home." As he said these words, he opened his own book and studied it briefly. "My book is also directing me to continue to Mount Thelema."

"But—but why would Sir Wisdom tell us that King Emmanuel wanted us to return home?" Gavin asked. "Sir Wisdom would never lie."

"Perhaps Sir Wisdom did not tell us that," Malcolm replied quietly.

"What do you mean?"

Katherine spoke up. "I have heard tales of a wicked enchantress who has the power to transform herself into any person or animal. Her name is Morphina. Perhaps it was Morphina who told us to return home."

Gavin ran back to the shaded glen. The clearing was empty—the old man was gone.

***

The sun was setting as the four tired travelers reached the base of Mount Thelema. The mountain loomed over them, titanic, thundering and threatening. Sheer cliffs rose above them like the walls of a massive castle. High overhead, the swirling clouds obscured the top of the mountain. "We can't climb that!" Aldith protested, tilting her head far back as she surveyed the jutting cliffs and ridges above them. "There's not a trail of any kind."

"I'm afraid that I have to agree with you, lass," Malcolm said slowly, as though it pained him to speak the words. "I see no way up. A mountain goat couldn't climb this."

A fiery bolt of lightning streaked across the skies and the resulting crash of thunder made them all jump with fright. Katherine looked up nervously.

Gavin opened his book and stepped toward the mountain. "The pages are glowing brighter than ever," he reported. "Emmanuel wants us to go this way." Guided by the book, he moved even closer. "Come look at this!"

Malcolm, Katherine, and Aldith hurried over and gathered around him. "What did you find?"

"There's a foothold," the young minstrel replied, pointing. "The trail up the mountain begins here."

"One step," Katherine scoffed. "Gavin, one step isn't going

to take us anywhere! We need a trail."

Gavin lifted his foot and stepped up into the depression in the rock. As he did, another foothold appeared. "Look!" he cried. As he stepped into the second foothold, a third appeared.

"There is a way up the mountain," Malcolm whispered in awe. "One step at a time."

"Can we camp here tonight?" Katherine asked. "I'm exhausted!"

Gavin nodded as he retraced his steps. "We won't climb the mountain in the dark," he declared. "We'll wait until the light of morning. But now we know that there is a way up the mountain."

Katherine surveyed the clearing. There were scores of tall, stately trees at the base of the mountain, but all had smooth trunks with no branches for the first sixty feet. "There is no wood to build lean-tos," she noted. "What will we do?" She glanced nervously up at the looming mountain where the lightning flashed and the thunder roared frightfully. "Perhaps it would be safer to camp farther from the mountain."

"We are following His Majesty's commands in coming here," Malcolm pointed out. "There is no safer place than right here."

Aldith already had her pack down on the ground and was searching through it. "Look," she said, pulling a roll of stiff broadcloth from her haversack, "what is this?"

"It's a tent," Malcolm replied, lowering his own pack to the ground to check it. "Emmanuel has provided tents for our use tonight. And I have one just like it."

Katherine and Gavin found similar tents in their packs. Within moments, the four tents had been pitched and camp was established. Gavin found a few sticks of firewood in his pack and built a fire. The sun dropped behind the ring of mountains to the west as the four weary travelers enjoyed a hot meal.

When the meal was finished, Katherine eyed the small, blazing campfire for a moment and then turned to Gavin. "Have you added any wood to the fire?"

Gavin shook his head. "There were only a few sticks in my pack. I used it all when I first built the fire."

"Then this is a miracle fire," she replied, pointing. "Your fire has been burning for half an hour, yet the wood has not been consumed at all."

"This has been a miracle quest," Malcolm said quietly. "I think all of us have seen the hand of Emmanuel at work as we have traveled."

Aldith sat quietly watching the stars. "Look," she whispered, "the stars directly above us form a perfect cross!" She nudged Gavin. "Can you see it? It's a perfect cross."

Gavin stared at her for a moment before answering. "Have you never seen that before? It's His Majesty's coat of arms." He pointed. "See, the cross that you see is in the center of a shield. Just above the cross is Emmanuel's crown. The whole constellation is Emmanuel's coat of arms."

Aldith was astounded. "It is," she murmured. "It really is! I wonder why I never saw that before."

"Many people miss Emmanuel's signs in the heavens, I suppose," he told her. "When His Majesty made Terrestria, he left his fingerprints on many parts of his creation. Have you ever seen the shepherd constellation?"

She shook her head.

He pointed. "There. To the north."

Aldith scanned the starry skies, spotted the shepherd, and gave an exclamation of delight. "It really is a shepherd! He's holding a staff, as if he is guiding a flock of sheep. That's spectacular—absolutely beautiful. And to think that I never saw these before."

"Emmanuel, the Great Shepherd," Malcolm said quietly. "The King who created such splendor is also the Shepherd who is willing to guide our lives. That's why we're climbing Mount Thelema tomorrow."

"Mount Thelema," Katherine said thoughtfully. "It's hard to believe that we're really here, that we're really this close to finding the will of our King. I wonder what his plans hold for me."

"We will find out very soon," Gavin replied. "Perhaps we should retire early and get all the rest we can. Tomorrow will be a difficult day, I am sure."

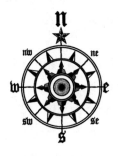

Chapter Twenty

"How much farther?" Katherine moaned. "Gavin, I can't take much more of this." Her plaintive voice echoed across the steep ravine.

Gavin gripped a tree root and looked back down the trail at her. The way was extremely steep and treacherous at that point, consisting merely of a series of jagged rocks that jutted from a sheer granite face, regularly spaced as if placed there to be used as steppingstones. The four travelers painstakingly made their way up the mountain by cautiously stepping from one projection to another, doing their best to ignore the empty chasm hundreds of feet below. One misstep would be fatal. The wind shrieked and howled as if determined to snatch them from the trail while lightning flashed overhead and thunder boomed ominously.

Gavin took a deep breath. His hands shook and his legs trembled, and he knew that his three companions were facing the same terrors. This was a place of danger, but the perilous trail was the only way to Thelema. "We'll rest when we reach the summit of this ridge," he called down to Katherine. "It's only another hundred feet or so."

"I don't know if I can make it," Katherine panted.

"Climb in the strength of King Emmanuel," Malcolm called to her. "His strength is our strength."

The woman nodded to show that she understood, but her face showed that she did not quite believe his words. Trembling with fear and exhaustion, she stepped across to the next rock.

"How are you doing?" Gavin called to Aldith, who climbed just below him.

"I'll be thankful when we reach the summit," she replied grimly. "I just wish the lightning and thunder would stop. And this wind is just dreadful."

Ten minutes later, the four weary travelers reached the crest of the ridge and gratefully found seats on various boulders. The wind still shrieked like a creature in pain and the thunder still rumbled, but for the moment, they were safe. Malcolm's hand trembled as he took a long, satisfying drink of water from his flask. "That was the most dangerous part of the entire quest," he remarked. "I hope the worst is over."

"Three days," Katherine replied. "We've been on the mountain for three whole days. How much farther, do you suppose?"

Gavin surveyed the mountainside above them. "In another hour or two we'll be in the clouds. Who knows what lies beyond?"

Aldith sighed. "I just hope we're doing the right thing."

"Doing the right thing?" Gavin stared at her. "We are following King Emmanuel's guidance on this quest. His book has led us to this point and we have all seen his provision for our needs and his protection in the times of danger. How can you question whether or not we are doing the right thing? We're doing this that we might know Emmanuel's will."

The girl shrugged. "True enough, we have seen Emmanuel's

provision and protection. But what if his will for us is not what we think it is?"

Gavin frowned. "What do you mean?"

"What if our King has plans for us that would make us miserable? What if his will is something that we cannot do, or cannot bear to do? We have been warned not to climb the mountain; that those who visit the mountain become slaves. What if...what if those stories are true?"

"I have been wondering the very same thing," Katherine admitted.

"We are trusting our King—" Gavin began, but Aldith interrupted.

"In truth, I have been filled with fear ever since we reached Mount Thelema," she told them all. "The lightning and the thunder never stop, and the wind seems determined to snatch us from the mountain and hurl us into one of the ravines! We have been in the midst of a storm ever since we set foot on this mountain. If this is the place that Emmanuel has chosen for us, why is it such a place of tumult and danger? I had hoped that Mount Thelema would be a place of peace and joy."

"We must trust Emmanuel," Malcolm interjected.

"That's becoming more and more difficult," Aldith replied. "The higher we climb, the worse the storm seems to get. What will it be like when we reach the summit—if we do reach it?"

Gavin sighed. "Do you want to turn back?"

Aldith shook her head. "I'm not sure what I want. I can't imagine getting this close and then turning back without finding Emmanuel's will. And I'm not looking forward to going back down; it will be worse than the trip up."

"Let's send petitions," Malcolm suggested quietly. "We have been so busy climbing that we have neglected to send messages to our King. Perhaps therein lies the source of our fears."

"Aye, you are right," Gavin replied sheepishly. "We have forgotten to send petitions."

As the others drew parchments from their books, Gavin took a parchment and wrote:

> "My Lord, King Emmanuel:
> We are nearing the summit of Mount Thelema, yet we find ourselves beset by fear and doubt, and there is talk of turning back. Strengthen us, my Lord, that we might reach the summit and find your will. Help us to trust and follow you whole-heartedly. Your son, Gavin."

Rolling the parchment tightly, he released it and watched as it disappeared into the clouds. Moments later, three additional petitions streaked across the top of the mountain. Gavin stood to his feet. "Are we ready to continue?"

"I am still fearful," Aldith confessed, "but I am ready."

Less than an hour later they entered the clouds. The dark mists swirled about them, thick and cold and intimidating, causing some of the old fears to return to haunt them. The path was wide enough at that point for them to walk four abreast, but the vapors were thick and obscured the trail, and they struggled to find the way. "Stay close together," Gavin told the others as he opened his book for guidance. "It will be easy to stray from the path in this fog."

A brilliant flash of lightning brightened the mountainside and the resulting crash of thunder made them all jump. "The higher we go, the worse the thunder seems to be," Katherine observed.

"Aye, but that dreadful wind has stopped," Malcolm replied. "We can be thankful for that."

"Turn back!" a shrill voice screamed from somewhere nearby, causing the four travelers to recoil in fright. "Turn back!

There is treachery ahead!"

Aldith paled and grabbed Gavin's arm. "Perhaps we should go no farther."

"This is a trick of Argamor's," Gavin replied fiercely. "Do not let him dissuade you from the quest."

"Turn back, turn back," a deep, grating voice warned, "for you will never make it. There is danger and death ahead."

"You will not prevent us from completing our quest and finding the will of Emmanuel," Gavin shouted at the unseen assailant. "We will not turn back, for we are trusting in his grace and climbing in his power. We will know victory!"

"You are doomed to failure," the voice insisted. "Failure and death lie ahead for all of you."

Suddenly the air was filled with a multitude of voices, all screaming and crying and shouting dire warnings about the dreadful fate that awaited them if they continued up the mountain. Terror engulfed the four travelers, wrapping its fiendish tentacles around them like a predator drawing its prey into a trap. "We must turn back!" Katherine cried out in terror. "We must turn back!"

"Trust in your King," Gavin admonished her, speaking in a loud voice to overcome the voices of terror. "His Majesty can keep you from harm."

"Turn back! Turn back!" the voices insisted. "Doom and disaster await you! Turn back, before it is forever too late!" Shrieks and wails and hateful voices filled the air, alternately coaxing and cajoling, then threatening and terrorizing.

"I cannot take any more!" Katherine cried in aguish. "I will turn back."

"Emmanuel, show yourself mightier than these," Gavin cried, "or Katherine is lost!"

"Sing praises," a quiet voice commanded, and at that moment, a sweet melody filled the air. Peaceful and gentle, the voice nevertheless overcame the harsh voices of fear and hatred that assaulted from every side. Gavin looked up to see the snowy white plumage of the dove.

"The name of Emmanuel is a strong tower," Gavin sang, and his rich baritone seemed to fill the atmosphere. "His name alone brings strength and power."

The myriad voices screamed again, but it was the woeful sound of the defeated and the vanquished.

"Sing with me!" Gavin urged his companions.

"Emmanuel's name, a place of rest," they sang in unison, "A refuge for Emmanuel's blessed."

"Keep singing," the young minstrel urged. "There is power in our praise."

Continuing to sing praises to their King, the four travelers advanced up the steep trail, victorious over the forces of fear and doubt. Katherine sang the loudest.

Moments later they stepped from the clouds and paused in astonishment. Before them stretched a wonderland of incredible beauty. "Would you look at that," Gavin said quietly.

"Incredible," said Malcolm.

"I've never seen anything so beautiful," Aldith commented.

"Thelema is a paradise," Katherine said, beaming with delight. "If Emmanuel's will is anything like this, it will be wonderful!"

"Can the Golden City of the Redeemed be this majestic?" Gavin wondered aloud. "This is incredible!"

Before them lay the summit of Mount Thelema, a vast meadow of incredible beauty, bright with life and promise. Flowering trees of all varieties adorned the meadow, living jewels of color and life. A crystal-clear stream flowed across the valley, its banks lined with wildflowers of extraordinary size and beauty, while the air was filled with butterflies and songbirds. Far in the distance stood an enormous building of glistening marble, beckoning to them with its gleaming white pillars. Above the breath-taking panorama hung a brilliant rainbow of seven glorious colors, bright and majestic.

Gavin held up one finger. "Listen."

Aldith touched his arm. "What is it?"

"The thunder and lightning have stopped."

At that moment, a brilliant beam of golden sunlight sparkled on the rainbow, reflecting back toward them in a cascading array of dazzling colors. Color filled the sky. An instant later, a chorus of powerful male voices filled the air, strong and melodious and thrilling. Another brilliant display of color shot from the rainbow, brightening the sky, to be followed an instant later by the answering chorus of men's voices.

Aldith turned to Gavin with a look of utter astonishment written across her lovely features. "It wasn't thunder and lightning!" she exclaimed.

The others stared at her. "What?" Malcolm blurted.

"It wasn't thunder and lightning that we heard and saw," the girl repeated. "The flashes of light that we saw were reflections from the rainbow and the thunder was actually the deep voices of the men's chorus that we are hearing."

"Listen," Katherine said, holding up one hand. "Do you hear women singing? Each time the rainbow sends out color and light, you can also hear the sound of a women's chorus, but you have to listen closely."

The four watched the skies and listened intently. Just as Katherine had said, the rainbow flashed and the sound of clear, high notes in perfect pitch resounded far in the distance. An instant later, the sounds of the men's chorus filled the skies. "It's the most beautiful music in Terrestria," Malcolm said reverently.

"Where do we go to find Emmanuel's will for us?" Aldith asked.

Gavin opened his book. "It's guiding us toward that building," he reported. He took a deep breath and let it out slowly. "This is the moment for which we have been waiting," he said, and his voice trembled. "Let's go."

As the four travelers made their way across the vast meadow, the glittering rainbow continued its dazzling display of color and light and the celestial music filled the air. "This is a place of peace and joy such as I have never known before," Aldith remarked. "Do you feel it, as I do?"

"King Emmanuel's will for us must be a plan of great peace and joy," Malcolm replied, "if just crossing Thelema is this fulfilling. Imagine what life will be once we know and follow his will."

Nearly twenty minutes later, the four travelers timidly made their way up a wide flight of glistening marble steps, amazed at the overwhelming size of the building. Columns twenty feet in diameter soared a hundred fifty feet into the air. Together the travelers made their way across a vast portico of polished marble and then passed through a double set of golden doors. Thoroughly intimidated by the vastness of the magnificent structure, they paused to find themselves at the edge of a chamber so vast that they could not see the far end. Rich draperies of exquisite purple graced the walls and were reflected in the polished floor of white marble. High above their heads, a translucent ceiling admitted the colors and lights from the rainbow above, creating dazzling displays of movement and color upon the glistening floor. In the center of the vast chamber stood a dais of solid gold, and upon the dais, an enormous throne of ivory inlaid with gold.

Music filled the vast chamber, rich and full and thrilling, and the four travelers instantly forgot their fears. The presence of Emmanuel was very real here, and they relaxed in the knowledge that he had summoned them.

"Faithful ones, approach the throne," a voice boomed from somewhere within the vast expanses of the great hall.

Glancing at his companions to reassure them, Gavin started for the dais, to be followed a moment later by Aldith, Katherine, and Malcolm. The swirling array of colors on the floor seemed to dance with joy.

"Come no closer," the voice called, when they were yet a hundred paces from the golden dais and the seemingly empty throne. The four travelers waited breathlessly.

"Emmanuel will reveal his will to one at a time," the voice informed them. "Malcolm the cobbler, approach the throne."

As Malcolm boldly walked toward the glistening throne, Gavin found that his heart was pounding as if it wanted out of his chest. What was about to take place would change his life forever.

Chapter Twenty-One

The music ceased as the cobbler crossed the vast marble floor toward the ivory throne. Time stood still. As Malcolm neared the golden dais, Gavin held his breath. Movement caught his eye and he looked up to see the dove soaring majestically on motionless wings. Ten paces from the dais, Malcolm abruptly fell to his knees.

"Malcolm, my son, you have learned to trust me." The powerful voice filled the vast chamber. "Your faith honors me and pleases my Father. You have come to Thelema seeking my will for you, and you shall not be disappointed. Since you have trusted me with your future, I have chosen the very best for you."

Malcolm waited expectantly.

Two beings arrayed in shimmering white robes appeared, bearing between them a large wooden chest. The voice commanded them to place the chest before Malcolm and open it, which they did. As the lid was raised, Malcolm gave an exclamation of amazement. The chest was filled to the top with treasure—gold, silver, and an array of glittering diamonds, emeralds, rubies, and sapphires.

Katherine gave a strangled gasp, and Gavin glanced toward her. The woman's eyes were wide and her limbs trembled.

"Incredible!" she whispered. "Never before have I seen such wealth."

"Malcolm, my faithful son, I give you the power to accumulate riches. You are skilled as a cobbler, and as a cobbler you shall serve me. Yet you shall become a cobbler such as Terrestria has never seen. The quality of your footwear shall become known far and wide and you shall soon hire many craftsmen to keep up with the demand for your shoes. In serving others by making quality shoes, you shall become wealthy.

"And yet, my son, you shall not waste your great wealth upon yourself, as many of the wealthy in Terrestria have chosen to do. You shall instead use your vast resources to further my kingdom: building castles for protection against Argamor, helping the poor of the land, and publishing my name across the kingdom."

Katherine gave another gasp as the glittering treasure vanished, leaving the chest empty.

"You do not need this wealth, my son, for I give you the power to generate your own. Be careful, for riches often seek to control and stifle their owners. Do not allow this to happen—remember that your great wealth is to be used primarily for the good of others and to build my kingdom."

The voice was silent. Malcolm waited anxiously. The two figures in the shimmering robes closed the chest, placed it before the trembling cobbler, and then vanished.

"Take the chest, my son, and return to your place with the others." Malcolm hoisted the enormous chest and rejoined his companions. His face was white, but his eyes shone with an inner happiness.

"Incredible," Katherine said softly. "I can't wait!"

"Gavin the minstrel, approach the throne," the voice commanded.

Gavin thought his heart would stop as he walked toward the golden dais and the ivory throne. Apprehension gripped him, and yet his soul was singing. Within moments he would know the will of King Emmanuel for him. Just as Malcolm had done, he dropped to his knees a short distance from the steps leading to the throne.

"Gavin, my son," the voice thundered, and the young minstrel found that the powerful voice was filled with love and compassion, "you have faltered on this quest, and yet you have prevailed. Your heart is yielded, and with that my Father and I are pleased."

The youth waited anxiously.

"At birth, you were given the gift of music. I have blessed you with a voice that is capable of blessing the hearts of your fellowman, yet for a time you wasted that gift upon yourself. From henceforth you will use that gift to honor me. I have yet two more gifts to give you."

Gavin turned and saw the two figures in white making their way across the vastness of the great hall. One was leading a magnificent roan stallion, while the other carried a golden lute. Gavin's heart beat faster.

"You will use the gift of music to draw your fellowman to me, and yet you will do far more than that, for you were also given the gift of words. You are a leader of men, and you will use that power to influence others for my kingdom."

"How am I to do that, my Lord?" Gavin's voice faltered.

"You are to travel across the regions of Terrestria as a minstrel. The horse will enable you to cover far more territory than you would afoot. Using your gift of music and your gift of words, you will proclaim the words of my book in order to draw many of Argamor's followers to become my children, and you will encourage my straying children to return to my side."

"Aye, my Lord," Gavin replied, and suddenly, his heart was overwhelmed with joy and gratitude. *Emmanuel's will for me is perfect,* he told himself. *How could I ask for more than this? I will spend the rest of my life glorifying Emmanuel with my music!*

The two shining figures approached, handing Gavin the lute and the reins to the horse and then vanishing as he accepted the gifts. Gavin's heart was singing as he walked back to rejoin his companions.

"Aldith, my daughter, approach the throne."

Aldith trembled as she walked across the vastness of the marble floor. Watching her, Gavin felt a surge of empathy. *Oh, that Emmanuel's plans for her will be as grand as his plans for Malcolm and me,* he thought wistfully. *My King, bless her as you have blessed me! Give her your best.*

Aldith was upon her knees before the golden dais.

"My daughter, at birth you were given the gift of great beauty, both inward and outward. Your heart longs to please me, and thus you are here today. Your faithfulness shall be rewarded.

"My daughter, I know your heart, and I know that you long for a home and children. I shall honor those requests. But first, I give you two gifts."

One of the white-robed attendants approached the trembling young woman bearing a decanter of crystal, which he handed to her. "I give you the gift of encouraging words," the great voice continued. "You shall use your words to be an encouragement to those around you, but especially to the husband that I shall give you. In his service to me he will face many trials and encounter many who would discourage him, yet you shall be a constant source of encouragement to his spirit and gladness to his heart. My daughter, guard this treasure with your life, for now there are those who would take it from you."

Trembling, Aldith gripped the decanter with both hands. "I shall, my Lord."

"And now for the husband," the voice continued. "Gavin, approach the throne and stand with this young woman."

Gavin was in a daze as he stumbled forward to stand beside Aldith. "My daughter, I have prepared your heart to serve as a help meet for this young minstrel. The life of a minstrel can be extremely difficult at times, and yet your words of encouragement will lift his spirits and strengthen his heart."

Gavin waited breathlessly. How would Aldith respond to the words of her King?

Aldith gave a cry of joy and threw herself into the arms of the stunned young minstrel.

The King's laughter filled the great hall. "Gavin, my son, will you have Aldith as your wife? You have seen her heart on this quest and you have seen her willingness to seek and serve me. Will you love her, provide for her, and protect her?"

"I will," Gavin replied softly, but his voice rang across the vastness of the great hall.

"Magistrate, bring the documents," the voice commanded. "Malcolm and Katherine will serve as witnesses to the ceremony."

One of the white-robed attendants approached with a parchment in his hand, and within moments, the marriage was complete. As the happy couple walked back to rejoin their companions, Katherine's name was called.

"My daughter," the King addressed the countess, as Malcolm, Aldith, and Gavin looked on from a distance, "years ago I blessed you and your husband with land and wealth. Yet you turned the blessing into a curse, for you squandered my gifts upon yourselves. You found out for yourselves that wealth does not bring happiness. Today I give you another chance at happiness, for I give you two gifts."

Katherine turned expectantly as the white-robed attendants approached. As she saw what they carried, her expression of anticipation turned to one of stunned horror. Her mouth fell open. She trembled as she was handed a sewing basket and a broom.

"My daughter, you will find your happiness as the servant of others. My gifts will enable you to make coats and garments for the widows and the poor, and to clean the homes of those who are unable to do so. If you accept my gifts, you will please my Father and honor me with your good works and almsdeeds."

Katherine was stunned. "B-but my Lord," she stammered, "th-this is beneath me! I-I am a countess, my Lord, not a s-servant!" The trembling woman choked on the last word.

"During my years upon Terrestria," the voice informed her, "I was a servant. Is the countess greater than her Lord?"

Katherine's face was a mask of fury. "My Lord, you gave my companions better than this," she stormed. "How can you give me, a countess, less than you gave them?"

"My precious child," the voice replied gently, patiently, "I saved the best for you. Oh, the rewards that are in store for you, once you reach the Golden City! Trust me, my daughter. You will remember that your life as a countess brought you no happiness, only misery and regrets. Your life as a servant will bring you joy such as you have never known."

To the amazement of Gavin, Aldith, and Malcolm, the furious woman turned and stormed from the great hall in silence.

"My Lord," Gavin called, "shall we bring her back?"

"Nay, for the choice is hers," the voice replied sadly. "Katherine must come to me of her own accord, or she shall never come at all."

"We rejoice to serve you, my Lord," Malcolm said. "May our hearts be yielded and may our lives honor you."

"And so they shall," the voice replied. "I have yet one more gift for each of you." At these words, the vast roof of the great hall suddenly split in the middle and began to open slowly like two enormous doors. Golden sunlight and brilliant colors filled the vast chamber. "You have wondered how you shall make your way back down the mountain, for the descent would be far more treacherous than the ascent. Fear not, for I have prepared a way for you."

At these words, thunder filled the skies above the building, echoing again and again within the great hall. Aldith looked at Gavin in disbelief. "Are we hearing thunder again?"

Four enormous winged creatures dropped from the skies on transparent wings of color and beauty. Alighting gently upon the glistening floor, they folded their mighty wings and the thunder ceased immediately. "Butterflies," Malcolm blurted in astonishment. "Butterflies with thirty-foot wingspans!"

"Actually, they are lepidopteras," Emmanuel's voice informed them. "They will carry you and your gifts back to your homes in the space of a few moments."

"His Majesty's will for me is perfect," Gavin told Aldith joyfully. "To think that I shall serve him as a minstrel is almost more than I can envision. And if that isn't great enough, he gave me the most beautiful woman in Terrestria as my wife!"

Aldith smiled sweetly. "And I am thrilled to have you as my husband."

"Emmanuel's will is best," Malcolm agreed. "I am so thankful that I left the choice with him!"

The lepidopteras began slowly opening and closing their great wings. Malcolm walked toward the magnificent creatures.

"How will Katherine get home?" Aldith worried.

"Katherine is in my hands," the voice replied. "She will wander in selfishness and self-pity for a time, yet I will continue to

BOOK ONE: TALES FROM TERRESTRIA

draw her to myself. If she will but yield her heart to me, I will bless her with the abundant life."

The lepidopteras were opening and closing their luminous wings faster and faster, flashing color and light across the great hall. The cobbler now sat astride the closest one, gripping the powerful muscles that attached the great wings to the body.

"Now go," the great voice commanded. "Go and fulfill my will, and you shall bring glory to my Father and be a blessing to others. Your lives shall be filled with great joy, for you have found the purpose for which you were created."

Hand in hand, Gavin and Aldith walked toward the waiting lepidopteras. Their eyes were filled with love and their hearts sang with joy. Mount Thelema, the land of music, color, and light, had changed their lives forever.

Epilogue

Three years later

The afternoon shadows were growing long as a powerful roan stallion galloped swiftly along the King's highway. The rider, a handsome young minstrel with a golden lute across his back, drew back on the reins and slowed his mount to a canter as he neared the gates of a little city. "Good day, my lord," he called cheerfully to a tall, well-dressed merchant just ahead of him, who was driving a heavily loaded freight wagon.

"And to you, sir," the merchant responded, guiding his team to the side of the road to allow the minstrel to pass. Their eyes met. "Gavin!" the merchant cried. "Gavin, is that you?"

"Malcolm?" The minstrel reined the magnificent horse to a stop. "Malcolm, I can't believe it!"

The merchant dismounted the wagon and the minstrel his horse, and the two men exchanged exuberant hugs. "Malcolm," Gavin cried, "how are you?"

"You're looking at the happiest man in Terrestria!" the merchant replied joyfully. "Ever since Mount Thelema, my life has been one of fulfillment and joy. Emmanuel's will is perfect, my friend, absolutely perfect! And to think that I almost turned back—I would have missed out on this life of adventure and delight."

Malcolm gripped Gavin's hand. "And how are you, my brother? How is Aldith?"

"You have to be the second happiest man in Terrestria," Gavin replied, with a twinkle in his eye, "for I am the happiest! Each day is now a thrilling adventure, a day of praise and great joy, for each day affords me the opportunity to serve my King. Aye, the quest for Mount Thelema was the greatest adventure of my life, for it opened the door to a life of peace and contentment such as I had never known! And Aldith—well, my lovely wife is the second greatest joy of my heart. Her presence fills me with happiness. Aye, together we are enjoying every moment of life, now that we are living in the will of our King. Right now I am on my way home to see my wife and daughter."

He grinned suddenly. "Oh, I forgot to tell you—Emmanuel has blessed us with a child, a little girl. In just a few days, she'll be a year and a half old."

"Emmanuel has been good to us," Malcolm said softly.

"Aye, that he has."

"Tell me about your travels. You are still a minstrel, I take it? I do see the lute upon your back."

"I am indeed a minstrel," Gavin said happily, "a minstrel in the service of the King of kings. I travel from town to town and from castle to castle, singing the songs of His Majesty and proclaiming the words of his book to those who will listen. I rejoice to tell you that I have been used to draw many folks to their King."

In his excitement, Gavin gripped Malcolm's doublet. "I tell you, Malcolm, this is the grandest life there is! Oh, that everyone in Terrestria would travel to Mount Thelema, learn the will of their King, and then serve him. What peace and joy they would find! What adventure, what fulfillment, what happiness they would know!"

Malcolm nodded in agreement. "Aye, lad, truer words were never spoken."

"So what about you?" Gavin inquired. "Tell me about your life since Mount Thelema."

"I cannot begin to describe the happiness I have found since we went on the quest," the cobbler merchant replied. "Mere words cannot describe Emmanuel's blessings upon me. Just as he promised, my King has smiled upon my calling as a cobbler. My business has expanded to the point that I now employ nearly a hundred craftsmen who do nothing except make shoes of the highest quality. I also employ nearly two score of merchants who travel across the kingdom, selling our shoes to those in need."

He paused reflectively. "Wealth beyond my wildest dreams has passed through these hands."

Gavin eyed the wagon. "I assume you have a load of shoes to sell?"

Malcolm smiled. "A load of shoes, aye, but to sell? Nay. I am delivering these shoes to a woman who will distribute them to the poor of the city. Come—you must meet her. Never have I known a woman with such a heart for the King. Some folks call her Dorcas, and some call her Tabitha, for she is just like the seamstress whose story is told in the King's book."

Gavin mounted the stallion and rode alongside Malcolm's wagon toward the city gate. "And what of Katherine? Have you heard news of her?"

Malcolm hesitated as if uncomfortable with the question. "Perhaps you will ask me later, lad."

Gavin said no more.

Malcolm reined to a stop before a humble daub-and-wattle cottage just inside the city gate. "This lady will thrill your heart," he promised, as he stepped down from the wagon. "To be in her presence is to be in the presence of Emmanuel himself. Never have you met a woman with a greater love for her King!"

Gavin dismounted and followed Malcolm to the door. The merchant knocked.

The door opened to reveal a slender peasant woman with long, dark hair that cascaded past her shoulders. Her simple gown was faded and patched but her eyes sparkled with happiness. Her face was radiant, giving testimony to a life of joy and fulfillment. Her eyes lit up when she saw the merchant. "Malcolm!"

"The shoes for the poor are here, Tabitha," Malcolm said, indicating the wagon with a sweep of his hand. "I will help you load them into the shed."

"Aye, and well-received they will be, Malcolm. We have quite a few garments ready, but the shoes are greatly needed. Emmanuel's blessings on you for your generosity."

Gavin stepped from behind Malcolm, and Tabitha's mouth fell open as she saw him. "Gavin?"

Gavin stared at the woman. There was something strangely familiar about her voice and her eyes. "Do I know you, my lady?"

Tabitha laughed, and her eyes crinkled merrily. "You should, Gavin, for we traveled together on a quest to Mount Thelema."

Gavin was speechless. "K-Katherine? Katherine, the countess?"

"Call me Tabitha," the woman requested, "for Katherine was a selfish, miserable countess. I would not stoop to be a countess, for now I am a happy servant to the King!"

Gavin shook his head in bewilderment. "The last time I saw you..."

"I was rebelling against the will of my king," she finished for him. "When I left the great hall of Thelema, I wandered atop Mount Thelema for several months, consumed with anger and self-pity. Even during my rebellion and selfishness, King Emmanuel graciously met my needs day by day. One day I realized that my King, in all his wisdom and love, knew better than I what was right for me. I trusted him and accepted his will for me."

A radiant smile lit her face. "Let me tell you, Gavin, the King's will was perfect for me! I have never been so happy in all my life. I wouldn't trade places with any countess in Terrestria."

"Tabitha makes garments for the orphans and widows of the city," Malcolm explained. "She has a volunteer crew of a dozen ladies who work together to clothe the poor." He opened the door wider, revealing three spinning wheels and a loom. "She is a blessing to this city."

"My King is using me," the woman said modestly. "Malcolm does much for the poor of this city, and other cities as well. He even offered to build me a grand house like his, but I declined his offer. This little cottage suits me just fine."

"Why would you not want a nicer house, my lady?"

"I am known as the happiest woman in this city," Tabitha said simply. "I want folks to know that my great happiness comes from serving my King, not from any possessions that I might own. Were I to live in a grand house like Malcolm's, perhaps folks would misunderstand the source of my great joy."

Gavin was thoughtful. "Not one of us would regret the quest to Mount Thelema, would we? In finding the will of our King, we found the abundant life—a life of adventure, of peace, and of great joy. Just think what we would have missed had we not gone on the quest for the thundering mountain."

Malcolm nodded. "Aye, lad, you are right. There is no greater joy than following our King."

Gavin looked up at the sun and sighed. "My friends, it is getting late and I regret that I must continue on my way. I am so grateful that we could meet again and hear of the great things Emmanuel is doing in each of our lives." The three friends embraced and bid each other farewell. Gavin mounted his stallion and cantered away.

Half an hour later, the weary horse and rider slowly passed a magnificent castle as a cool breeze swept down from the fells and the evening stars began to appear. Gavin glanced up at the massive walls and lofty towers and a thrill of delight swept across his soul. "Just think," he told the stallion, "in just three days I'll stand in the great hall of this very castle, doing what I love most—praising the name of King Emmanuel in story and song."

Shifting his weight in the saddle, the grateful young minstrel ran his fingers lightly over the strings of his lute and his rich baritone voice echoed against the castle walls. "I delight to do thy will, O my King;" he sang, "yea, thy law is within my heart..."

THE TERRESTRIA CHRONICLES

Have you read the companion series, The Terrestria Chronicles?

Want to share them with your friends?

The Sword, the Ring, and the Parchment

The Quest for Seven Castles

The Search for Everyman

The Crown of Kuros

The Dragon's Egg

The Golden Lamps

The Great War

All volumes available at

WWW.TALESOFCASTLES.COM